THE YOUNG FIREMEN OF LAKEVILLE

OR HERBERT DARE'S PLUCK

FRANK V. WEBSTER

1st WORLD
LIBRARY
Literary Society

The Young Firemen of Lakeville

Frank V. Webster

© 1st World Library, 2006
PO Box 2211
Fairfield, IA 52556
www.1stworldlibrary.com
First Edition

LCCN: 2006909911

Softcover ISBN: 978-1-4218-3333-0
Hardcover ISBN: 978-1-4218-3233-3
eBook ISBN: 978-1-4218-3433-7

Purchase *"The Young Firemen of Lakeville"*
as a traditional bound book at:
www.1stWorldLibrary.com/purchase.asp?ISBN=978-1-4218-3333-0

1st World Library is a literary, educational organization
dedicated to:

- Creating a free internet library of downloadable ebooks

  - Hosting writing competitions and offering book
    publishing scholarships.

Interested in more 1st World Library books?
contact: literacy@1stworldlibrary.com
Check us out at: www.1stworldlibrary.com

1ˢᵗ World Library Literary Society

Giving Back to the World

"If you want to work on the core problem, it's early school literacy."

- James Barksdale, former CEO of Netscape

"No skill is more crucial to the future of a child, or to a democratic and prosperous society, than literacy."

- Los Angeles Times

Literacy... means far more than learning how to read and write... The aim is to transmit... knowledge and promote social participation."

- UNESCO

"Literacy is not a luxury, it is a right and a responsibility. If our world is to meet the challenges of the twenty-first century we must harness the energy and creativity of all our citizens."

- President Bill Clinton

"Parents should be encouraged to read to their children, and teachers should be equipped with all available techniques for teaching literacy, so the varying needs and capacities of individual kids can be taken into account."

- Hugh Mackay

CONTENTS

CHAPTER I

A MIDNIGHT ALARM

"Fire! Fire! Turn out, everybody! Fire! Fire!"

This cry, coming like a clarion call, at midnight, awoke the inhabitants of the peaceful little New England village of Lakeville.

"Fire! Fire!"

Heads were thrust out of hastily-raised windows. Men and women looked up and down the street, and then glanced around to detect the reddening in the sky that would indicate where the blaze was. Timid women began sniffing suspiciously, to learn if it was their own homes which, unsuspectingly, had become ignited.

"Fire! Fire! Stimson's barn is burning! Fire! Fire!"

A man ran down the principal village street, shouting as he ran. At some doors he paused long enough to pound with his fist, awakening the dwellers who had not heard his call, for he was Rodney Stickler, the town constable and watchman, whose duty it was to sound the fire alarm, and summon the bucket brigade, in the event of a blaze.

"Hurry up!" Constable Stickler shouted, as he ran from house to house, striking with his fist on the doors of the residences where the members of the bucket brigade lived. "The barn is 'most gone! Fire! Fire!"

Men jumped from bed, pulled on shirts, trousers, and shoes or boots, and thus scantily attired, rushed forth to do battle with the flames.

In a small cottage, near the end of the village street, a lad, hearing the midnight alarm, got up and hurried to the window. He could make out the short, stocky form of Constable Stickler rushing about. Then, off to the left, he could see a dull glow in the sky. There was, also, the smell of wood burning.

"What is it, Herbert?" asked a woman's voice from another room.

"Fire, mother," replied Herbert Dare. "Mr. Stickler is giving the alarm."

"Whose place is it? I hope it isn't around here. Oh! fire is a dreadful thing! Where is it, Herbert?" And Mrs. Dare put on a dressing-gown and came into her son's room.

"I think he said it was Mr. Stimson's barn, mother. I can see a blaze over in that direction."

"Mr. Stimson's barn? He has a fine lot of cattle in it. Oh, I hope they save the poor creatures!"

Herbert, or, as he was usually called by his chums, Bert, grabbed up his clothes from a chair, and began to sort them in the darkness, looking for his trousers.

"What are you doing, Herbert?" asked his mother.

"I'm going to dress."

"What for?"

"I'm going to the fire."

"Herbert! Don't go! You might get hurt. Suppose some of the horses should run away and trample on you? Don't go!"

"I must, mother. They'll need all the help they can get. I must go!"

From the village street once more came the alarm.

"Fire! Fire! Fire!"

Now, however, more voices were shouting it. There was also the rush of feet, and Bert, peering from the window, saw a crowd of men and boys, many of them carrying buckets, hastening along. The glare in the sky had become brighter.

"I'm going to dress and go, mother," said the boy. "I want to aid all I can. We'd like help if our house was on fire."

"Oh, Herbert! Don't suggest such dreadful things!"

Mrs. Dare left her son's room, and in a few minutes he had dressed sufficiently to go out.

"Now do be careful, Herbert," called his mother, as he ran downstairs. "If anything should happen to you, I don't know what I'd do."

"I'll be careful."

Herbert Dare was the only son of a widow, Mrs. Roscoe Dare. Her husband had died several years previous, leaving her a small income, barely sufficient to support herself and her son. It may be added here that Mr. Dare had been a city fireman before his marriage. This, perhaps, accounted in a measure for the interest Herbert took in all alarms and conflagrations.

"It certainly looks like a big fire," thought the boy, as he broke into a run down the street. He soon caught up with the crowd hastening to the blaze.

"Hello, Bert!" shouted a lad to him. "Going to help put the fire out?"

"If they need me, Vincent. I see you have your bucket."

"Yep," replied Vincent Templer, one of Bert's chums. "It's dad's. He belongs to the bucket brigade, but he's away from home, and I took it."

"I wish I had one."

"Oh, I guess they'll have plenty at the barn."

"They'll need 'em, for it looks as if it was pretty well on fire."

The reflection of the blaze was now so bright that objects in the street could be plainly seen, and faces easily distinguished at a considerable distance.

"There's Cole Bishop!" said Bert to his chum, pointing to another lad, who was running along, evidently much out of breath, as he was quite fat.

"Hello, Cole!" called Bert.

"Hello—Bert! Goin'—to—the—fire?" came from Cole, with a puff between each word.

"Naw, we're goin' to a Sunday school picnic," replied Vincent, who was something of a joker.

"Humph! Funny—ain't—you!" remarked Cole.

The boys continued to speed on toward the burning barn, which was one of the buildings belonging to Anderson Stimson, a farmer, and located just on the edge of the village.

The crowd had increased, and several score of people were on their way to the conflagration.

"They'll—have—a—hot—time—putting—out—that—fire," spoke Cole, with labored breath. "They—only—got—buckets."

"That's all they've had in Lakeville since the time it was founded by Christopher Columbus," remarked Vincent. "It's a good thing we don't have many fires."

"If I had my force pump I could show—show—'em—how—to—squirt—water," said Cole, who had begun the first part of the sentence very fast, but who had to slow down on the last section. He was almost completely out of breath.

"Why didn't you bring it along?" asked Bert.

"Huh! How—could—I—when—it's—fast—on—the—cistern?"

That argument was, of course, unanswerable. Cole Bishop was a lad quite fond of mechanics, and was usually engaged in making some new kind of machinery. His force pump was his latest effort, and he was quite proud of it.

"Say! I should think it was burning!" suddenly exclaimed Bert, as he and his chums turned a corner of the street and came in full view of the blazing barn. The structure seemed enveloped in flames, great tongues of fire leaping high in the air, and a black pall of smoke hovering like an immense cloud above it. "They can't save that!"

"Guess not!" added Vincent. "What good are buckets in a blaze like that? You can't get near enough to throw the water on."

"Wish—I—had—my—force—pump," panted Cole.

By this time the boys had joined the crowd that was already at the scene of the fire. The heat could be felt some distance away.

"Come on, everybody with buckets!" cried Constable Stickler, who sometimes assumed charge of the bucket brigade. "Form a line from the horse trough to the barn. Pass the full buckets up one side and the empty ones down the other. Let the boys pass the empty buckets an' the men the full ones."

"Let's form two lines for full buckets," proposed another man.

"We'll need three," put in a third individual.

"Who's runnin' this here fire, I'd like to know?" inquired the constable indignantly. "Git to work now."

"Yes, I guess they'd better, or there won't be any barn to save," spoke Bert.

The flames were crackling furiously. The crowd was constantly increasing, and nearly every man had a bucket or pail. Some had brought their wives' dishpans, as they could not find their pails in the darkness and confusion.

"Come on, Bert, let's get in line," suggested Vincent.

"Yes—let—me—git—to—a—place—where—I—can—rest," begged Cole.

"Here, I'll help," added John Boll, another of Bert's chums.

"I'd rather pass the full buckets," said Tom Donnell.

"Now then, everybody begin to pass," cried the constable, who had his men in some kind of shape. There were three lines extending from the burning barn to the horse trough, some distance away. The trough was fed by a pipe, running from a spring, and there was plenty of water.

"Dip an' pass," cried the constable, and the word went along the lines. Men standing near the trough dipped their pails in, handed them to the person standing next, and so, from hand to hand went the dripping buckets of water. At last the pail reached the end of the line, and the man nearest the blaze proceeded to throw on the quenching fluid.

But here a new difficulty presented itself. The blaze was so hot that no person could approach close enough to make the water effective. The whole front of the barn was in flames.

"This ain't going to be no good!" exclaimed one of the men on the end of a line up which the full buckets traveled. He tried to throw the water on the flames, but, approaching as close as he dared, he could not come within ten feet of the fire.

"I should say not," agreed his companion.

"Hey! What's the matter?" called the constable. "Why don't you throw the water on the flames, instead of on the ground?"

"Let's see you do it," was the angry answer.

"We'll have to go around to the back, and throw the water on there," was the advice of a tall, lanky farmer.

"What good'll that do?"

"Wa'al, we can't do no good here."

"That's so," was the general agreement.

The lines began to shift, to get out of the heat of the blaze. Meanwhile, those at the trough, not understanding what was going on, continued to pass up the full buckets, but as no one gathered up the empty ones to pass back, the waiting line of boys had nothing to do. Several began to leave, to get in a position where they could view the blaze better.

"Here, where are you boys going?" demanded Constable Stickler, who was running back and forth, not knowing what to do.

"There isn't anything for us to do," replied Bert. "We can't save that barn with buckets. We'd better help get some of the machinery and cattle out."

"That's right," added Vincent, and several men agreed with this.

"You—ought to have my force pump," spluttered Cole Bishop, who had now recovered his breath.

"Pass up the buckets! Pass the buckets!" was the cry that now came from the line of men, that had been extended to reach around to the rear of the barn, where, for the time being, there was no fire. "Pass the buckets!"

"Yes, pass the buckets!" shouted the constable. "Here, boys, come back to your places!" For a number of the boys had left, and there were long gaps in the line.

"Can't something be done to save the barn?" cried Mr. Stimson, who had been rushing back and forth, mainly engaged in carrying out some valuable harness from the blazing structure.

"We're tryin' to," replied the constable.

"Are all the cattle out?" asked Bert.

"Cattle? Land, no; I forgot all about them!" exclaimed the farmer. "I was busy taking my valuable harness out, and saving some of my deeds and mortgages in the house. I'm afraid that'll go next!"

"The house is in no danger as long as the wind keeps this way," said Bert, "but the cattle are. How many are in the barn?"

"Five horses and six cows. The cows are in the lower part. They're in no danger yet, but I guess the horses are done for. I forgot all about 'em!"

At that moment a shrill cry, almost like a human being in agony, rose above the crackle of the flames.

"Those are the horses!" cried Bert. "Come on! We'll try to save 'em!"

CHAPTER II

IN PERIL

Accompanied by several men and boys, Bert ran toward the barn. The whole front, and part of the roof, were now blazing. The structure was beyond saving, as far as anything the bucket brigade could do, but the members of that primitive fire department did not stop.

The buckets were passed from hand to hand, but such was the haste that a full bucket seldom reached the end of the line. Usually about half the fluid was spilled. And what little did get there was merely tossed against the side of the barn that was not yet burning, though from the way it was smoking it would evidently not be long before it burst into flames.

Once more came the frightened neighing of the horses, tied in their stalls. Their cries were weird and terrifying, for a horse seldom gives expression to its fear in that manner.

"You can't get 'em out!" called Constable Stickler, who had heard what had been said. He left his supervision of the bucket brigade and ran alongside of the boy. "The fire's all around 'em. You can't get 'em out!"

"Well, I'm going to try," declared Bert.

"My fine horses!" exclaimed Mr. Stimson. "This means a terrible loss to me!"

Frank V. Webster

"Is the barn insured?" asked the constable.

"Yes, but my stock ain't. Oh, this is a terrible calamity! An awful misfortune!"

Bert approached as closely as he dared to the blazing front of the barn. Clearly no one could enter that way. But he knew the structure well, for he had once helped Mr. Stimson get in his hay, when a shower was threatened.

"Come around to the side door!" he called to those who followed him, and, such was the effect of his leadership, that no one now thought of questioning it. In times of excitement one cool head can do much, and Bert was cool.

Beside the main entrance to the barn, which was up an elevated driveway, there was a door opening into a sort of basement, and from that, by means of stairs, the main floor of the barn, where the horses were, could be reached. This door was locked, but Bert smashed the fastening with a big stone, since Mr. Stimson was too much excited to remember where the key had been placed.

"Come on!" cried the boy.

"You can't take the horses down these stairs," said the constable, as he and several other men followed Bert.

"No. Don't try it," added the farmer. "They'll break their legs."

"I'm not going to," said Bert. "Couldn't if I wanted to. The stairs are too narrow and steep. Hey, Cole," he called to his chum, who with Vincent had left the now utterly useless bucket brigade lines, "you slip around and let out the cows. Mr. Stimson, you'd better show him."

"That's right. We'll git the cows out!"

The cows were kept in the basement of the barn, the entrance to it being on the other side, level with the ground. The flames had not eaten down, as yet, and the cows were found patiently chewing their cud. It did not take long for Mr. Stimson and his neighbors to get them out.

With the horses it was a more difficult matter. These highly nervous animals, half maddened by the fire, were running about, having now broken their halters, and they could be heard trampling on the floor overhead. Part of the floor was burning, and the animals were confined by the flames to one side of the barn.

"You'll never git them out," prophesied the constable.

Indeed, Bert was beginning to have his own doubts. But he had a plan which he wished to try.

"Come on, Vincent," he called to his chum. "You know how to handle horses, don't you?"

"Sure."

By this time the two boys and the constable had reached the head of the stairs, and were inside the barn, on the main floor. Fortunately the flames were not yet near the stairway.

"Look out for the horses!" yelled Mr. Stickler. "They're crazy with fear!"

The animals certainly were. Back and forth they rushed as the shifting flames and smoke drove them from place to place. The interior of the barn was becoming hotter and hotter. Most of the front had burned away, and through it, wreathed in flames and smoke as it was, those inside could look out and see the wondering crowd gathered before the structure.

"Goin' to drive the horses through?" asked Vincent.

"No. They'd never cross those burning embers," replied Bert, pointing to where pieces of blazing wood had fallen across the threshold of what had been the big doors of the barn. There was a wide zone of fire, and from it the frightened horses shrank back, though, once or twice, they seemed about to make a rush across it to safety.

"How you goin' to do it?" asked the constable.

"Look out!" suddenly called Vincent. "They're coming right for us!"

The maddened creatures, frightened by a puff of smoke that surged down from the now blazing roof, charged, like a small troop of cavalry, right at the two boys and the man.

"Down into the stairway!" cried Bert, making a dash for the place they had just come up. They reached it just in time. The horses thundered past, huddled together, avoiding by instinct the narrow, steep stairs, down which, had they stumbled, they would have met their deaths.

"Now's our chance!" cried Bert. "While they're in the far end of the barn!"

"What are you going to do?" asked Vincent.

"Open those other big doors!"

The barn had two sets of large doors. Only one pair was used, however, those up to which the elevated driveway led. The others were to give air to the place, when hay was being stored away, and they opened right into the cow-yard, ten feet below, with a sheer drop over the threshold.

"Do you think those horses will jump out there?" asked the constable.

"I think they will, rather than burn to death."

"But the jump will break their legs."

"Not a bit of it. The cow-yard is soft and mucky. They will sink down in it, and the men can lead them out. Come on, Vincent, help me open the doors." Bert's plan was now evident, and it seemed feasible. But would the frightened horses leap to safety?

Running up from the stairway, in which they had crouched when the horses thundered past, the two boys hurried across the barn to the big doors. Constable Stickler called out:

"I'll go and send some men around to the cowyard."

"All right," replied Bert.

He and Vincent were almost at the doors when, once more, the horses came at them with a rush. The boys were in great peril, but Bert saw their chance of safety.

"Jump up on the mowing machine!" he yelled, and he and his chum crawled upon the apparatus just in time. So close were the horses that one of them stumbled over the extended tongue of the machine, and fell. It got up in an instant, however, and joined its companions, that stood trembling in a corner, staring with terrified eyes at the flames that were eating closer and closer. The barn floor was smaller than it had been, for the fire was consuming it, foot by foot.

"Come on, now!" cried Bert, and a moment later he had thrown aside the heavy bar that held the doors in place, and had swung them open. The draft, created by the fire, served to hold them so.

"Now help me drive the horses out," he called to Vincent. "Get behind them, but look out they don't turn on you."

Cautiously the two boys made their way to where the terrified animals were. Their mere movement was enough to send the

Frank V. Webster

horses off on the run again. Fortunately the leader smelled the fresh air coming in through the opened doors. The horse paused a moment on the threshold and seemed to be staring down into the partly illuminated cow-yard. Would he jump?

"Go on, old fellow!" called Bert, encouragingly. "Jump! You won't hurt yourself. It's soft mud. Go ahead, old fellow."

Whether the horse understood, or whether the boy's words calmed him, could not be told. Certainly he did jump, after a moment's hesitation, and a glance back at the flames which were coming closer and closer.

The other animals followed in an instant, for they had wanted only a leader. Above the roar of the flames Bert could hear the thud as the horses landed in the soft muck of the cow-yard, ten feet below. Then came a shout as the men rushed forward to secure them.

Bert looked from the big double doors. He could see the horses floundering around. One had fallen down, but none of them seemed to be injured. The valuable steeds had been saved by the lad's ready wit.

"I wonder if there's anything more we can save?" asked Vincent.

"Let's see if we can't shove out the mowing machine," suggested Bert. "If it falls in the muck it can't be damaged much."

The two boys shoved the apparatus to the opened doors. Another shove and it toppled over and out. It landed safely, as they learned later.

"Come on, here are some bales of hay and straw. Might as well save them, too," suggested Bert. "The fall won't hurt them, and the men can roll them out of the way before the flames reach them."

They managed to save several bales, all they could reach; and they also rolled out a carriage, which, as it had the bales to topple out on, falling only a short distance, was very little damaged.

"That's the stuff, boys!" called Constable Stickler, who with a crowd of others was in the cowyard, removing such things as the boys pushed or tossed out, for they found many small objects they could save.

"There isn't much more we can get out," called Bert in answer. "It's getting pretty hot here. Guess we'll have to leave, now."

He and Vincent turned to descend the inner stairs, by which they had entered. As they did so there was a crash, and the forward part of the roof fell in. An instant later the stairway was buried put of sight under a mass of blazing wood.

"We can't get out that way!" cried Vincent. "We're caught in a trap!"

"The big doors!" replied Bert. "We can jump out, just like the horses did."

"That's so! Come on! I guess the mud won't hurt us!" They turned to that side of the barn, but to their horror they saw a stream of fire pouring down over the opening, as a cataract of water flows over the edge of a fall. To escape they would have to jump through the flames.

CHAPTER III

TALKING IT OVER

What had happened was this. There was loose hay and straw in the upper part of the barn. The flames, eating up and along the roof, had burned into this, until the whole mass was ablaze.

Then, as the upper part of the side of the barn, above the big open doors, was burned through, the burning hay and straw began falling into the cowyard. Right down it fell, like a cataract of fire.

It made a pile in the muck of the cow-yard, whence the men had led the horses, wheeled out the mowing machine and carriage, and removed the baled hay and straw.

At first the blazing wisps were extinguished, as the cow-yard was wet, but, as more and more of the hay and straw fell, there gradually grew a pile of blazing hot embers. But, worse than all, was the curtain of fire that shut off escape by the big doors.

"What are we going to do?" asked Vincent, his face white with fear.

"We are up against it," replied Bert, speaking more calmly than would have been possible for most lads. But Herbert Dare was unusually cool-headed, a fact which later stood him in good service.

"Maybe the stairs are safe now," suggested Vincent.

It needed but a look at them to show that they were almost burned away.

"No escape there," decided Bert.

"Isn't there an end door?"

"One, up in the loft, but it's thirty feet from the ground and that's too much of a jump. Besides, we can't get into the loft now. It's a mass of flames."

"Then we've got to jump through the big doors and take our chances with the fire!" declared Vincent.

"Wait a minute," advised Bert.

He looked about him, seeking some means of escape. It would be dangerous to try to leap through the doors. They would fall into a mass of burning straw, which would scar them terribly, as would also the falling cataract of ignited wisps. Yet there was no other way.

Then a daring idea came to Bert. He remembered reading about a man who once escaped in a similar manner from a burning barn.

"Grab up a horse blanket!" he called to Vincent. There were several scattered about the barn, and they were of heavy wool.

"I've got one," shouted Vincent. At the same time Bert found a large one.

"Dip it in water," was the next command.

In one corner of the barn, near the horse stalls, there was a pump, at which were filled the pails to water the horses when they were in the barn. There was water in one pail now.

Bert dipped his blanket in, and drew it out dripping wet. But the wool had absorbed most of the water, and there was only a little more left in the pail.

"Here, wrap this about you, and jump!" cried Herbert, passing the wet blanket to his chum, and taking the dry one from him.

"What will you do?"

"Never mind about me! I'll pump some more water. You jump, before it's too late!"

Outside could be heard confused shouting. It was the crowd, calling to the boys to hasten, as the roof was about to fall in. There were anxious eyes waiting for the reappearance of the two young heroes.

"Jump! Jump through the big doors!" yelled Bert, helping Vincent to wrap the blanket about his body, and fairly shoving him toward the only available avenue of escape. "Jump! It will be too late in another minute!"

Above the crackle of the flames could be heard men yelling:

"Come on, boys! Come on! The roof's going!"

With a look at his chum, Vincent pulled the blanket more closely about him, leaving only a small opening near his face through which he could look. Then he ran to the big doors.

Bert stuffed his blanket into the pail, in the bottom of which was a little water. Then he began to work the pump to get more.

He gave one glance, saw his chum leap through the big opening, with the curtain of fire, and then, murmuring a hope that he was safe, he began to work the pump-handle. To his horror no water came. The fire had eaten down into the cow stable, and melted the pipe that ran from the pump to the cistern. No water was available to wet his blanket, on which he depended to save himself from the flames.

"Bert! Bert! Come on! Jump!" he heard some one call.

He caught up his blanket It was merely damp.

"It's got to do!" he murmured. "I'll be scorched, I'm afraid, but there's no help for it! Here goes!"

Wrapping the covering about him, he dashed across the barn floor. It was ablaze in several places under his feet. The cataract of fire was now fiercer than ever over the opening of the big doors. Holding the blanket to protect his head, he took a running start, and jumped.

Straight through the big opening he went, and he heard a confused cheer and shout as he appeared. He felt the hot breath of the fire all about him. He smelled the scorching wool, the burning straw and hay. His nose and mouth seemed full of cinders. He felt himself falling down, down, down. He tried to keep himself upright, that he might land on his feet, but, in spite of himself, he felt that he was turning on his back. He twisted and squirmed, as does a diver who wants to cleave the water cleanly. Oh, how Bert wished he was diving into the old swimming hole, instead of into a fiery mass of straw and hay!

He landed on the ground in a crouching position. He seemed to be smothering in a mass of black cinders that rose up in a feathery cloud all about him. He could hardly breathe.

Then he felt some one grab him—several hands began carrying him forward. An instant later his blanket was unwrapped from his head, and he found himself in the midst of a crowd of men and boys.

"Look out! The blanket's afire!" some one called, and Constable Stickler kicked the burning mass of wool to one side.

Suddenly there was a great crash, and the roof of the barn toppled in. A great shower of sparks arose, and there was a dense cloud of smoke. Then the flames seemed to die down, for there was little left for them to feed on.

"You got out just in time," said Vincent, coming up to Bert, and grasping him by the hand. "Did you get burned any?"

"Just a bit; on one hand. I had to leave it out to hold the edges of the blanket together. How about you?"

"Not a scorch, but I'm wet through from the blanket. It saved me, though."

"The pump wouldn't work," explained Bert. "But come on, let's get out of this. I'm standing in mud up to my knees. Why, the pile of burning straw and hay that was down here seems to be out."

"Yes. I yelled to the bucket brigade that they'd better use the water on this, instead of throwing it against the sides of the barn, where it wasn't doing any good. So they did, and they kept a good deal of the fire down, so's you'd have a good place to land in."

"I owe that to you, Vincent."

"And I owe my wet blanket to you, so we're even. But let's get on dry ground."

The cow-yard, with the natural wetness that always existed there, to which had been added many gallons of fluid from the bucket brigade, was now a miniature swamp.

The boys, followed by an admiring throng, made their way to the front of the barn. All work at attempting to save it had now ceased. Nothing more could be done, and, as all the cattle and horses had been saved, as well as some of the wagons and machinery, it might be said that all that was possible had been accomplished.

"Got to let her burn now," said the constable. "How'd it start, Mr. Stimson?"

"Tramps must have sot it, I guess. Fust I knowed I woke up, an' see th' blaze. Then I sent my boy Tom out to yell."

"Yes, I heard him," replied the constable. "He yelled good and proper. I got right after the bucket brigade." "That's what you did."

"Well, the bucket brigade might as well have stayed in bed for all the good it did," remarked Cole Bishop, who had recovered his usual calmness. "You'd ought to had a couple of force-pumps like mine."

"Oh, you boys clear out," advised the constable. "First thing you know you'll git hurt."

"Huh! I guess if it hadn't been for some of us boys, there'd be a bigger loss than there is," retorted Cole.

"That's so," agreed Mr. Stimson. "Bert and Vincent saved me several hundred dollars by getting out them horses."

"Any of 'em hurt?"

"The bay mare's a little lame, from jumpin', an' the roan gelding is scratched on the fore quarter. But, land! that's nothin'. They'll be all right in a day or two."

"Pretty heavy loss, ain't it, neighbor Stimson?" asked Mr. Peter Appelby, who lived next to the man whose barn was now but a mass of glowing embers.

"Yes, 'tis, but I got insurance. I'm glad it wasn't the house."

"Guess you kin be. Land! but it did go quick! I never see such a fierce fire. I sure thought them two boys would be burned to death," remarked Nate Jackford, another neighbor.

"So did I," admitted Mr. Stimson. "It's been a terrible night."

"But it might have been worse."

"That's so."

There was nothing more that could be done. The horses and cows were taken in charge by several neighbors, who agreed to keep them until Mr. Stimson could build a temporary barn. Then, as there was little more to see, for the barn was now completely consumed, the crowd began dispersing.

"Lakeville ought to have a fire department," said Bert, as he walked home with his chums.

"Yep. They need some force-pumps like mine," agreed Cole. "I got a hose rigged up on it, an' if our house got afire, I could put it out as easy as pie."

"Yes, it's a good pump of yours," admitted Vincent, "but what we need here is a regular pumping engine, and some lines of hose. If we'd had 'em to-night we might have saved the barn."

"The Selectmen of Lakeville are too stingy to appropriate any money for a fire department," said Bert. "I remember once, years ago, when my father was alive, he proposed it, but nothing ever came of it."

"This is a miserly town, anyhow," added Cole. "They never have any Fourth of July celebration."

"That's right," agreed his chums.

Little was talked of in the village the next day but the fire at the barn. Bert and Vincent were praised on all sides, and when Bert appeared in the streets, with one hand bandaged up, where it had been slightly burned, he was congratulated by nearly every one who met him, until he blushed like a girl.

"If Constable Stickler had given the alarm a little earlier, so's the bucket brigade could have got there quicker, we could have saved the barn," said Moses Sagger, the owner of the only butcher shop in town. He was a member of the brigade.

"That bucket brigade could never have put out that fire, Moses," said Peter Appelby. "There wasn't water enough."

"Yes, there was. Didn't we put out the fire at Sim Rockford's, one day, about two years ago?"

"Yes, but that was only his henhouse, when his wife put a charcoal fire in it to keep the hens warm so's they'd lay more. That wasn't much of a blaze. Besides, it was in the daytime, and we had the brook to get water from."

"Well, the bucket brigade's good enough for Lakeville," declared the butcher. "What's the use of talking? I've seen it do good work."

"Well, maybe once in a while. But it can't handle a big fire. We need a regular department, that's what we do."

"What, and increase the taxes to pay for it? I guess not much!" exclaimed Mr. Sagger. "I pay too high taxes now. The bucket brigade is good enough."

"That's the kind of men that keeps Lakeville from growing," thought Mr. Appelby, as he walked off. "He's too miserly to want to pay a few dollars extra each year to support a regular fire department. But we'll have to have one some day."

That day was nearer than Mr. Appelby supposed.

CHAPTER IV

BERT HAS A PLAN

Lakeville was a typical New England village. It was of fair size, and was located on Green Lake, hence the name. There was also a small river which emptied into the lake, and which ran around one edge of the town. Altogether it was a very nice place, but, like many other towns, the principal citizens lacked a progressive spirit.

The town was governed by ten men, called the Selectmen, who were elected each year, and who formed a sort of council. Then there was a mayor. At the time this story opens Mr. Appelby was mayor, and Moses Sagger was chairman of the Selectmen. Mr. Sagger had an ambition to be mayor the next year, and he was working to that end.

"Well, Herbert," said Mrs. Dare to her son at dinner the day following the fire, "I hope you don't get up to go to any more midnight alarms."

"Why, mother?"

"Because I was worried to death about you. I knew you would get hurt, and, sure enough, you did."

"Oh, this burn? That doesn't amount to much. I'm glad I went, for I helped Mr. Stimson save something from the fire."

"Yes, I heard about it. All the neighbors are talking about you. You certainly take after your father, and I am quite proud, though I can't get over how frightened I felt."

"I'm sorry you feel that way, mother, for I was thinking of a plan that might save the village from any more such fires, and I might have to take part in it"

"What do you mean, Herbert?"

"Well, I think the village ought to have a fire department, a volunteer one at least, and I was thinking of organizing it."

"Well, Herbert, you know your poor father used to say the same thing, but he never could get any one to agree with him. The men don't seem to take an interest in such a matter, though I should think they would."

"I wasn't thinking of taking in the men, mother."

"Not take in the men? Whom would you have, then?"

"The boys—my chums."

"What! your friends—the boys you play ball with?"

"Yes. I think we could organize as good a fire department as if we had the men, and I'm sure we could get out quicker on alarms, and could beat the bucket brigade all to pieces."

"I'm afraid that's too big an undertaking for you boys, Herbert. Maybe the men will get together, now, and do something, after this barn fire. Perhaps they'll organize a department."

"I don't believe so. I heard that Mr. Appelby and Mr. Sagger were talking about it, and Sagger and his crowd object to spending the money."

"That's another point, Herbert. You'd have to have money to run a department."

"Not much. You see we boys would serve without pay, and all we'd need would be an engine."

"But engines, even the kind worked by hand-pumps, cost money."

"I know it, but we might get a second-hand one cheap. We could raise the money somehow—get up a show, or have a ball game."

"Perhaps you might, Herbert. But I don't want you running into danger. I'm sure you are thoughtful to take so much interest in the affairs of the town. Your father used to be that way."

"Well, our house might catch fire some day, mother, and if I belonged to the boys' volunteer department, we could put it out for you in a hurry."

"Don't suggest such a thing, Herbert. I'm afraid we'll never have a department here."

"Stranger things have happened, mother. I'm going off now to see some of the boys."

Though this was the first time Bert had spoken to his mother about his plan of organizing a fire department in Lakeville, he had been thinking over the matter for some time. Even before the barn burned down he had had the 'notion in his head, and, when he saw the futile efforts of the bucket brigade, he determined to take some action.

As he strolled down the village street, on the lookout for some of his chums to whom he might broach the subject, he espied Cole Bishop.

"Hello, Bert!" called Cole. "How's your burn?"

"It's getting better. What you going to do?"

"Nothing special. What are you?"

"Same thing, I guess. I was looking for some of the boys."

"What for? Going swimming or fishing?"

It was the vacation season, school having closed about a week previously.

"Well, I wasn't exactly going swimming, but I want to talk about water."

"About water? Say, you ought to see my force-pump. I put some new washers in it, and it'll squirt fifty feet now. Come on over. I wish our house would catch fire."

"You do? What for?"

"Well, I'd show you how to put it out. I've got my pump on the cistern, and some hose ready to attach. It's got the bucket brigade beaten a mile."

"That's what I want to find some of the boys to talk about, Cole. I'm thinking of organizing a fire department."

"A fire department! Say, that's great! I'll belong, and I'll let 'em use my force-pump—no, I can't, either. It's fast to the cistern." "I guess we'd need something a little larger than that, if we have a department," replied Bert, "but you can join, and we'll let you fix the engine pumps when they get out of order."

"Will you, really? Say, that's immense!"

"There's Vincent, now," went on Herbert Dare, as he saw his chum who had aided him at the barn blaze.

"Yes, and John Boll is with him. Hey, John! Hi, Vincent! Here she comes!" and Cole threw a ball high in the air towards the other two boys. John caught and returned it.

"Come on over here," called Cole. "Bert has a great scheme."

The four boys were soon in earnest conversation. Bert told of his plan for getting as many of the village boys as possible to join a volunteer fire department to answer all alarms.

"Where are you going to get the engine?" asked John.

"And where's the money coming from?" inquired Vincent.

"That's all got to be thought out," replied Bert. "Maybe Cole can make us an engine. He makes almost anything."

"That's so," came from John.

"Guess I'll have to wait a few years before I can make a fire engine, though," responded Cole. "But say, I just happened to think of it! They've got a new chemical engine over to Jamesville."

"I don't see how that helps us," said Bert.

"Don't you? Well, listen. If they've got a new engine, they won't need their old hand-pumping one."

"Well?"

"Don't you see what I mean? They'll sell the old machine and we can buy it. It's a good one, and has a fine pump on. All it needs is a little fixing, and I can do that. What's the matter with buying the second-hand engine of Jamesville?"

"Nothing's the matter," returned Bert slowly, "except that we haven't got the money."

CHAPTER V

BUYING THE ENGINE

This announcement served like a dash of cold water to the boys. They had been quite enthusiastic over Cole's plan, but Bert's words made them realize that it was one thing to say what they would do, and another to accomplish it.

"I—I guess we'll have to give it up," said John Boll. "It would be lots of fun for us boys to have a department, but I'm afraid we can't."

"It wouldn't be altogether fun," said Bert, "as we'd have to work hard to put out fires. But I don't know that we'll have to give up the plan. I wanted to talk to you fellows, and see how you felt about it. Perhaps we can raise the money."

"How?" asked Vincent.

"Well, we could give some sort of an entertainment, get up a ball game, and charge admission, and we boys can make some cash doing odd jobs, and put that in the treasury."

"I believe the folks in this town are too mean to come to a show or a ball game, even if it was to help buy an engine, and a second-hand one at that," declared John.

"We'll give 'em the chance," replied Bert. "But, fellows, what do you think of the plan?"

Frank V. Webster

"What plan is it?" asked a new voice, and the boys looked up to see Tom Donnell.

"We're going to have a fire department," declared Cole, and he proceeded to tell what they were discussing.

Tom was enthusiastic over it, as, indeed, were all the boys. Several other lads came along, until there was quite a crowd of them, and Bert was kept busy explaining his scheme.

From his butcher shop near by, Moses Sagger looked at the knot of earnestly talking lads. To him that meant but one thing.

"Them boys is hatching some mischief," he said to his helper. "They're going to play some trick, I'll bet an apple."

"And I guess it's a rotten apple at that," thought Sidney Balder, who worked for Mr. Sagger. "He's too mean to bet a good apple."

"Better keep your eyes open for them boys," went on the butcher. "They'll tip over one of my barrels of potatoes outside, or throw mud in on my floor, or something. Guess you'd better bring in all the stuff from outside, until they go away."

"I don't believe they'll touch anything, Mr. Sagger," declared Sidney, who did not fancy having to bring in all the boxes and barrels from in front of the shop, and take them out again.

"Yes, they will! I know boys! They're always playing tricks. Bring the things in."

So Sidney had to do it, laboring hard, and all to no purpose, for no sooner had he brought the produce in, than Bert and his chums passed on down the street, not bestowing so much as a glance at the butcher shop. They were too occupied thinking of the prospective fire department.

"There, I'm glad they're gone," said Mr. Sagger. "They made me nervous standing there. Put the things out again, Sid."

The boys, at Cole's suggestion, had adjourned to his barn. He had a double object in inviting them. He wanted to have a comfortable place to sit down, while they talked the matter over, and he wanted to demonstrate his improved force-pump.

This pump was the pride of Cole's heart. He had made it out of parts of several old pumps, and, to give him credit, it did throw quite a stream, when the handle was vigorously worked. The boys admired it to his entire satisfaction, and even admitted that it would be of good service if ever Cole's house caught fire.

"Now, let's talk business," Bert proposed. "Cole, do you know about how much the authorities at Jamesville would want for their old engine?"

"I haven't the least idea, but I should think they'd sell it cheap."

"Do you know whether they will sell it?" asked Tom.

"No, not for sure, but I should think they would."

"We can't go by that," declared Bert. "We've got to find out for sure."

"I move that Bert and Cole be a committee to go over to Jamesville, and see if they can buy the engine," sang out Vincent. "That'll start things going."

"Why, we haven't got our fire department yet," objected Charlie Rupert.

"What's the good of a department if you haven't got an engine?" replied Tom Donnell. "I'm in favor of that motion."

"So am I!" cried a number of the boys.

"We haven't regularly organized," said Bert, who was rather pleased at the enthusiasm of his chums, "but I'll be willing to go over to Jamesville and see what we can do. Cole can look at the pumps, and see if they will work well."

"Yes, they can't fool me on pumps," declared the owner of the improved forcing apparatus on the family cistern.

Thus it was decided, though there was enough more talk about it to fill several books the size of this one. Bert and Cole promised to go over to Jamesville the next day, and report back to their chums, in Cole's barn, the following night. Jamesville was a village about five miles from Lakeville, but more progressive in every way than its neighbor.

Bert and Cole made the trip the next day. They inquired at the Jamesville post-office as to whom they might approach in the matter of buying the second-hand engine, and were referred to the chief of the small fire department.

That individual received the boys cordially. He was a man much interested in fighting fires, and he was justly proud of the new chemical engine the town had purchased.

"Will they see the old engine?" asked Bert anxiously, after they had been shown the new one.

"Yes, the town committee voted to dispose of her to anybody that wants her."

"How much?" And at the question the hearts of the boys beat anxiously.

"Sixty dollars, and it's very cheap. It cost three hundred when new. It's got double-acting pumps, and there's two hundred feet of good hose. It's dirt cheap."

It was. Cole, who knew something of machinery, admitted this, and Bert had hardly hoped to get anything in the shape of an engine for less than seventy-five dollars.

"Do you boys want to buy it?" asked the chief, for Bert had told him the object of their visit.

"We did, but we haven't the money. Could the engine be held for us, for a few weeks?"

The chief looked thoughtful. Then he told the boys he hardly believed this was possible, as it was not certain they could raise the cash, and, in the meantime, a sale to some other party might be lost.

But the chief sympathized with the boys. He took them around to the chairman of the town committee, and the result of the visit was that the official agreed to hold the engine for a week for the Lakeville boys. If they could raise twenty dollars by that time they could take the engine, and agree to pay the rest in installments.

Bert and Cole talked the matter over. They thought this was possible, and they agreed to it. The result was they hurried back to Lakeville, with a written option on the engine, good for one week.

Their chums were hastily summoned, the matter talked over, and the boys went down in their pockets for whatever small sums they had saved up. The total was only eight dollars, but Bert proposed that they get up an exhibition ball game and charge admission.

This was done, and, by hard work, doing all the odd jobs they could find, the boys just managed to raise the twenty dollars, having made seven at the ball game.

"Let's get right over to Jamesville, the first thing in the morning," proposed Cole, after the contest was over and he and Bert were counting up the proceeds. "Maybe they'll sell it to some one else."

"Our time isn't up for two days."

"I know; but they might forget. Well start early."

They did, and before noon had completed arrangements, paid the twenty dollars, signed an agreement to pay forty more, and were told they could take the engine.

CHAPTER VI

THE FIRST RUN

"How are we going to get it home?" asked Cole, as he and Bert, with the Jamesville fire chief, went out to look at the hand engine. It was in a shed, back of the place where the new chemical machine was housed.

"Can't you borrow a horse and drive it over?" asked the chief.

"No; let's get the fellows over here and pull it back to Lakeville," proposed Bert. "That'll be fun. We'll wake up our old town by parading through it."

"That's the idea," agreed the chief. "Your citizens need stirring up, anyhow. That was quite a fire you had over there the other night. If you'd had a chemical engine like ours that blaze could have been put out."

"That's what it could," replied Cole.

"I had a visit from one of your men the other day," went on the chief.

"Who?"

"Mr. Sagger. He wanted to know, in case they had a bad fire in Lakeville, if we'd lend 'em our engine."

"What did you tell him?" asked Bert.

"I said we were always willing to help our neighbors, but that we wouldn't lend our new engine. I asked him why they didn't have some sort of a department, instead of a bucket brigade, but he said they were poor, and couldn't afford it."

"Why, he's worth lots of money," declared Cole. "He could support a department himself, and never miss the cash!"

"Did he say anything about our boys' department?" asked Bert.

"Yes, he mentioned it; but he laughed at it. Said it was only a lark of you lads, and would never amount to anything."

"We'll show him!" exclaimed Cole. "Maybe he'll be glad of our service, some day."

"I like the spirit you boys show," went on the chief. "If I can help you, give you advice, or anything like that, why, don't hesitate to call on me."

They thanked him, and promised that they would. Then they again began to discuss how to get the engine back, and finally decided to get their chums, make a trip for it, and haul it back in triumph that afternoon.

A hand fire engine, as probably many of my young readers know, is just what the name implies. In the days before steam engines were invented, one manner of putting out fires was by hand engines.

The hand engines of those days, and the one which the Lakeville boys had purchased, was nothing more or less than a big tank on wheels, with a pump to force the water from the tank through a hose. The water was poured into the tank by pails, so that a sort of bucket brigade was really necessary. Then there was needed many pairs of strong arms to work the pump handles, or "brakes," as they were sometimes called.

These handles were quite long, and usually there were two of them, arranged something like those on a hand-car, used by construction gangs on a railroad. There was thus room enough for several men or boys to take hold of the poles on either side of the engine.

Sometimes those working the handles stood on the ground, or, in case of a large engine, like the one the boys had purchased, on top of the water tank. The water was poured into the tank at one end and forced out at the opposite end, through the hose. On some engines there were two lines of hose, and very powerful pumps, but, of course, the efficiency of the engine depended on the amount of water it could throw, and this, in turn, depended on how fast the bucket brigade could fill the tank.

When the tank was full and sturdy arms were working the long handles up and down, there was a steady clank-clank to the pump, and a stream could be thrown for some distance. The engine was hauled to fires by means of a long double rope, which, when not in use, could be reeled up, as could also the hose.

Some of those old hand engines were very elaborate affairs, with brass work and shiny lamps on them, and they were gaily painted. The one the boys had purchased had been a fine machine in its day, but was rather battered now. Still, it was in good working order, and had a long length of hose.

"I'll tell you what let's do," suggested Cole, as he and Bert were on their way to Lakeville, to get their chums; "let's wait until after dark to bring it into town, and then we can light the lanterns on the machine," for there were four, one on each corner.

"Good idea!" replied Bert. "We'll do it. And we'll march down the main street, singing. I guess that will make a stir."

The plan met with instant endorsement on the part of their

chums. They got together as many boys as they could, and late that afternoon the crowd went to Jamesville. The engine, which had been put in good shape, was ready for them.

"Look out you don't lose the buckets," cautioned the chief. "They're hanging underneath the tank. Now, boys, good luck, and may your first run be a success."

They thanked him for his good wishes, and the lads, having grasped the long rope, set out, dragging the engine after them. They made good time, and soon were on the outskirts of Lakeville.

"Now, wait until I light the lamps," said Bert, as it was getting dark. "Then we'll start through the town, singing. Sing for all you're worth!"

The boys needed no urging. They were full of enthusiasm over the new plan, and when the lamps were lighted on the old engine they gleamed on the brass work, making it sparkle brightly.

"It looks almost as good as new!" exclaimed Cole. "And them pumps is fine. They're almost as good as my force pump."

"Oh, let up on that force pump, can't you!" asked Tom Donnell. "You'd think it was the only pump in town!"

"It's the only one of that kind," declared Cole, a little hurt that his "patent" should thus be spoken of.

"All ready, now, boys?" asked Bert.

"All ready," was the general response.

They started off. Above the rumble of the wheels of the engine rose their voices in song, and, as they entered the main street of the village, people began to come out to see what the unusual excitement was about, for the purchase of the engine was not generally known, few persons believing the boys were serious in organizing a department. "It's a circus!" exclaimed a little girl.

"Naw, it's one of them Indian medicine shows," declared Moses Sagger, who stood on the steps of his butcher shop.

"Why, it's a fire engine!" exclaimed several men. "However in the world did the boys get it? They must have borrowed it to have some fun with!"

"More likely took it without permission," said Mr. Sagger. "Somebody ought to tell Constable Stickler."

Down the street marched the proud boys, singing at the tops of their voices, the lamps showing off the engine to good advantage.

"Well, I must say those young chaps have a lot of gumption!" declared Mr. Appelby. "I wonder if they're going to keep the engine?"

"I wish there was a fire—I mean a little one, that wouldn't do much damage," said Cole. "I'd like to show 'em how she works."

"We might have arranged a bonfire in some lot and given an exhibition," suggested Bert, "We'll do that, after we have our company regularly organized."

But the boys were destined to give an exhibition before they anticipated it.

From down toward the end of the village street there came a cry.

"Fire! Fire! Fire!"

It was Constable Stickler's voice.

Frank V. Webster

"Fire! Fire!" he yelled. "Kimball's haystack is on fire! Turn out the brigade!"

It was a quiet evening, and his voice carried a long distance. The boys heard it plainly.

"Come on, fellows!" cried Bert. "Here's our chance! The engine is in good working order, and we'll have our first run!"

CHAPTER VII

BERT SAVES A TRAMP

The boys needed no further call. With whoops and yells they began to haul the engine rapidly in the direction of the fire, the reflection of which could already be seen.

"Come on!" cried Mr. Sagger, to several of the bucket brigade. "We must put out the fire. Come on, men!"

He caught up his bucket from the corner where he kept it. Other villagers did likewise, and soon there was quite a throng headed for the burning haystack.

"Leg it, boys! Leg it!" cried Tom Donnell. "Don't let those fellows of the bucket brigade get ahead of us!"

"If-they-do-we-can-beat-'em-by-squirting-more-water," panted Cole Bishop. "But-say-fellows-go-a little slower-I can't-run-much farther."

Indeed, he was out of breath, for the long tramp from Jamesville had tired him.

"Jump up on the engine, Cole," proposed Bert. "We can pull you. We'll make you engineer, and the engineer always rides on the machine."

"All—right," responded Cole, gratefully. He scrambled up on

Frank V. Webster

the apparatus, and, with a shout and cheer, the boys were off faster than before, for Cole had been a hindrance rather than a help, in pulling the apparatus, as he could not go fast.

"Fire! Fire!" shouted many voices, taking up the cry of the constable.

This brought out nearly all the members of the bucket brigade. The blaze was now brighter.

"Where we going to get our water?" asked John Boll of Bert, as he raced alongside of his chum, both dragging on the rope.

"In the brook. It runs right past Kimball's place, and we can form a line of buckets right down to it and up to the engine."

Mr. Kimball's place was on a side street. He had a house and a small barn. The latter building was not large enough to store his hay in, so he kept the stuff in a stack outside.

"Come on! Come on!" Constable Stickler could be heard yelling. "The barn'll catch pretty soon."

"We're coming!" replied Bert.

"For th' love of tripe! What's that?" cried the constable, as he caught sight of the engine.

"The Lakeville Fire Department!" responded several boys.

"Humph!" exclaimed the constable. "Don't you boys go to interferin' with the bucket brigade. I won't have it. The bucket brigade is the regular department for this town."

"The only thing the matter with it is that it can't put out any fires," was the retort from John Boll. "Let's show 'em how we do it, boys."

On the way from Jamesville, Bert and Cole, who had been

instructed by the chief of that department how to operate the engine, imparted this information to their chums. So, though the lads had never before worked a hand engine, they felt that they could make a good showing.

"We'll have to hustle, boys," called Bert to his little force. "That bucket brigade will have it in for us, and they can handle a haystack fire pretty good. Let's show 'em how we do it."

By this time they had turned down the side street to where the burning hay was. The flames had mostly enveloped it, and Mr. Kimball and his two sons were vainly dashing pails of water at the base of the ignited pile.

"Run the engine right down to the brook," said Bert. "We won't have to pass the water so far then. As soon as it stops I'll unreel the hose and Cole will call for some fellows to jump up and work the handles. Don't have any disputes. The rest will pass buckets, and John Boll and Tom Donnell can handle the nozzles. I'll pass water, this time."

The post of honor, of course, was at the nozzles, of which there were two. Next to that came being at the handles, or brakes, while the hardest work and probably the least spectacular was passing the water. Bert deliberately selected this, as he knew putting out the fire depended entirely on the water, and he did not want it said that he chose the best position, as he wanted plenty of lads to assist him with the buckets.

"This way, bucket brigade!" called Mr. Sagger, who acted as a sort of chief at times.

"Here you are with the engine," cried Bert, in opposition. "Right down to the brook, boys!"

"Form lines!" directed Mr. Sagger. "Pass buckets."

Bert and his chums ran the engine close to the stream of water.

Then Burt unreeled the two lines of hose, and gave them in charge of Tom and John. Cole was busy oiling the brake bearings and calling for ten boys to assist him. The others, with Bert, grabbed the buckets from where they hung underneath the tank, and ran toward the brook.

In less than three minutes from the time they had the engine in place, the boys at the handles could pump water, so quickly was the tank partly filled.

"Now, boys, keep her as near full as you can," advised Bert.

There were many willing hands. Into the tank splashed pail after pail of water. Up and down went the long handles, with a "clank-clank." The flattened lines of hose filled out as the water squirted through them, and an instant later, out from the nozzles spurted vigorous streams, which Tom and John aimed at the blazing stack.

There was a loud hissing, as the water struck the hot embers, and a great cloud of steam arose.

"That's the stuff!" cried Bert, from his position near the brook. "We'll have it out in a few minutes."

"Pass the buckets faster!" cried Mr. Sagger. "Douse out the fire!"

The members of the brigade had not been idle. They had formed two lines, one for the empty and one for the filled pails, and the end man at the latter line was kept busy tossing gallon after gallon of water on the fire. But his was slow work compared with that of even the primitive hand engine. He had to stop, momentarily, after each bucketful, to reach for another and to toss aside the empty one.

Then, again, he could only throw water on one spot at a time, and this only a short distance above the ground, whereas most of the fire was near the top. But the hose lines could be aimed to send the water high into the air, whence it descended in a shower, wetting the stack all over.

Such vigorous treatment could have but one effect. In a little while the fire was under control, save at one place, and this was opposite the line formed by the bucket brigade. The young firemen had refrained from directing water from their lines there, as they did not want to wet the men.

"Douse the blaze there!" cried Mr. Kimball, as he saw that in spite of the good work of the boys much of his hay might yet be burned.

"Don't you dare do it!" cried Mr. Sagger to John and Tom. "We can put this out."

"Why don't you do it, then?" inquired the owner of the hay. "You've been long enough at it. Here, I'll do it."

He made a grab for the nozzle Tom held, and in doing so doused Mr. Sagger.

"I'll have you arrested for that!" cried the butcher. "You done it on purpose!"

"Wa'al, I'm going to have this fire out!" replied Mr. Kimball, and a few seconds later, with the aid from the other nozzle, the blaze was comparatively out. It still smouldered a bit on top, but a few sprinkles from a hose quenched that.

"Fire's out!" cried Cole, from his place on top of the engine. "How's that for the new department?"

"Boys, you're all right!" exclaimed Mr. Kimball. "There ain't more than half my hay burned. If I'd waited for that bucket brigade it would all be gone!"

"That's not so!" cried Mr. Sagger. "We'd have had it out in five minutes, if those lads hadn't interfered with us."

Frank V. Webster

"That's right," added several men, who did not like the praise accorded to the young fellows.

In spite of the good work they had done, there was not the best of feeling toward the boys on the part of the members of the bucket brigade. But on unprejudiced observers the work of the young firemen made a good impression, and they were warmly praised.

Quite a crowd had collected around the engine, examining it by the light of the four lanterns. All the boys were there save Bert, and he had remained near the brook to gather up some of the engine buckets that had been dropped there.

As he was picking them up he saw some one crossing the little bridge that spanned the stream, over a hole that was quite deep. The bridge had no side rails, and the figure, which was that of a man, seemed to be unfamiliar with this fact.

As Bert watched he saw the man sway toward the edge, and, an instant later, topple over into the water, where there was quite a swift current.

"Help! Help!" the man cried. "I'm drowning!"

Bert hesitated only long enough to toss off his coat and in he plunged. He could just make out the head of the man, being swept under the bridge, and he swam rapidly toward it. An instant later he had caught the man by his rather long hair and was pulling him toward shore.

"You—you saved my life!" gasped the rescued one, as soon as he was on the bank and could speak, for he had swallowed some water. "I can't swim."

"Oh, I guess you'd have been all right," said Bert. "It is shallow a short distance below here, and you could have waded out."

"No," said the man, rather solemnly; "I'd have gone to the

bottom and stayed there. I'm that unlucky."

He seemed quite affected and spoke sadly. Then, by the distant gleam of the lanterns on the engine, Bert saw that the man was ragged and quite unkempt. In short, he was a tramp.

"Where are you from?" asked Bert.

"From New York. I was asleep under that haystack, and I woke up to find it on fire."

"Were you smoking there?" asked Bert, suspiciously.

"No," replied the tramp, so earnestly that Bert believed him. "I don't smoke. But I was traveling with a fellow who did. Maybe it was his pipe that set the fire. He ran off, and I stayed around to see you boys put out the fire. You did it in great shape. I started to cross the bridge and I fell off. I'm weak, I guess. I haven't had anything to eat all day."

"Where are you going?" asked Bert, for he felt a sympathy for the man. No one else had been attracted to the scene, as every one was too much interested in the new engine to leave it.

"I don't know," replied the man, despondently, "I'm looking for work."

"What do you do."

"I'm a stenographer and typewriter, but there are so many girls at it now that a man can't get living wages. So I decided to become a tramp. I wanted to get out doors, because my health is not good. But I can't get anything to do, except very heavy tasks, and I'm not able to do them."

"I'll see if I can't help you," proposed Bert. "Come with me. I can give you a bed for the night."

"No, you've done enough for me. You saved my life, and I'm

grateful. Some day, maybe, I can return the favor. I'll go on now. If I stayed around here they might arrest me on suspicion of setting the hay on fire. I'll keep on. Maybe something will turn up."

"Then take this money," said Bert, handing the tramp a quarter. "You can get something to eat with it."

CHAPTER VIII

ON THE LAKE

The tramp seemed overcome by emotion. He held the quarter which Bert had given him as though he did not know what to do with it.

"It's a good one," said the lad, with a smile.

"Oh, I wasn't thinking that," was the answer. "It—it seems queer to have any one decently civil to me, that's all. I tell you, I appreciate it, young fellow. I've had a hard time of it. Maybe it was mostly my own fault, but I certainly have had hard luck. I can't afford to work for the wages they pay girls, and since I had to give up my job I've been down and out. Nobody had a decent word to say to me—especially since my clothes got to looking so bad."

"I wish I could do something else for you," said Bert. "But I haven't any more money. You see, we boys are trying to pay for that engine."

"Oh, I wouldn't accept any more of your money. It makes me ashamed to take this, when I'm a grown man, and you're but a lad. I tell you, when I fell in the water I didn't much care whether I came up again or not."

"That's a wrong way to feel."

"I know it, and I'm going to get over it. I'm going to make a new start, thanks to you. I'll not forget you. Maybe you'll see me when you least expect it."

With this the tramp turned away, crossed the little bridge, this time in safety, and hurried off across the fields, as he saw several of the boys coming down toward the brook.

"That's a queer tramp," thought Bert. "I wonder if I ever shall see him again?"

He was destined to, and under strange circumstances.

"Hello, Bert!" cried Cole, who was one of the group of boys. "What are you doing here? The fire's all out."

"I know it. I was gathering up the buckets. Guess we'd better get the engine back home—that's another thing we hadn't thought of. Where are we going to keep it?"

"My barn's a good place," replied Cole. "That will give me a chance to fix some of the pump valves. They didn't work just right to-night. Why—hello! You're all wet!" he added, as he came close to his chum, and saw that his clothes were dripping water.

"Yes-er-I-cr-I got in the brook," replied Bert, not caring to tell about the tramp just yet.

"I should say you did get in. Some of the fellows must have left the buckets too close to the edge. But, come on, let's haul the engine back."

Most of the crowd had now dispersed, a few members of the bucket brigade lingering to further examine the engine, while some of them made slighting remarks about it. The boys paid no attention to them, but, taking hold of the long rope, pulled the machine through the main street of the village. The lads found their new fire department increased largely as they advanced, for not a youngster in town, whether or not he had before this taken an interest in the organization, but who was now glad to get hold of the rope and pull.

"Guess we could organize two companies with this crowd," remarked Cole, looking at the throng.

"Yes. We'll have to get together to-morrow or next day and elect officers. Then we'll have to arrange some sort of a plan for answering alarms."

The engine was run into Cole's barn, and the boys crowded around for another observation of it. They actually seemed to hate to leave it to go home to bed. "Say, I guess it isn't going to run away," remarked John Boll, at length. "It'll be here tomorrow and the next day. I'm going home."

This started the boys to moving, and soon Cole shut up the barn, taking extra good care to see that the doors were locked.

"Maybe some members of that jealous bucket brigade might take a notion to run our engine off," he said to himself.

But no such calamity happened, and the machine was safe in the barn in the morning when Cole overhauled the valves and fixed them. Bert and some of his chums called around after breakfast, and they talked fires and engine to their hearts' content.

In the next few days several meetings were held, and the Boys' Volunteer Fire Department of Lakeville was formally organized. Because of his part in starting it, Herbert was unanimously elected captain. There was a little contest as to who should be the lieutenant, but the honor went to Vincent in recognition of his good work at the Stimson barn fire.

Of course, Cole was made engineer, chief mechanic and everything else that pertained to the actual operation of the engine. He was about the only boy who could qualify, for only he could take the pumps apart and get them together again. Tom Donnell was made chief of the "bucket corps," as the boys decided to call that part of the fire-fighting force whose duty it was to keep the engine tank filled with water. The other boys, to the number of a score or more, were made ordinary firemen, to help haul the engine, pass the buckets or work the handles.

There was some dispute as to who would be in charge of the hose, at the nozzle ends, during a fire, and, to get around this, as it was considered a post of honor, Bert decided the boys could take turns. There was something fascinating about directing a stream of water upon a blaze, and it is no wonder that every boy but Cole wanted the place. That is, excepting Bert, and he had all he could take care of with his duties as captain.

It was decided to keep the engine permanently in Cole's barn, as that was near the centre of the village.

"We ought to have some sort of an alarm bell," suggested John Boll. "We can't always depend on Constable Stickler."

"That's so," admitted Bert. "I wonder if we couldn't get permission to have the church bell rung?"

This seemed a good idea, and Bert and Cole interviewed the minister on the subject. He readily agreed to let the bell on the edifice be rung whenever there was a fire, and it was arranged that a long rope would hang from the belfry to the ground outside, where it could be reached by the constable and pulled to give an alarm. Mr. Stickler was delighted with his new office and increased duties.

"I'll have a regular signal system," he explained to the boys, after studying over the matter at some length. He had lost all his antipathy to the engine, and now favored the new fire department more than he did the bucket brigade. "I'll ring the bell once when there's a fire in the northern part of the town," he said; "twice when it's in the east, three times when it's in the south, and four strokes when the blaze is on the west side."

The boys were pleased with this plan, and also delighted that the old constable took such an interest in their work. As for the members of the bucket brigade, they, for the most part, sneered whenever the new department was mentioned.

"Wait 'till they get up against a real fire," said Moses Sagger. "Then we'll see what good their old second-hand engine is. They'll have to depend on the bucket brigade then."

The matter of paying the remaining forty dollars due on the engine worried Bert and his chums not a little, until Cole's father suggested that they charge a small sum weekly for each boy who belonged. As every youth in town was anxious for the honor, it was figured that they could collect at least a dollar a week in this way, since they charged each boy five cents, and there were over twenty. Then, too, at Mr. Bishop's suggestion, they decided to ask a donation from every person whose property they helped save from the flames.

Mr. Kimball, whose haystack was partly saved, heard about this, and sent the boys five dollars. Mr. Stimson, in view of the good work of Bert and Vincent, sent the new department ten dollars, so they began to see their way clear, especially as the Jamesville authorities voted to give the boys as long as they needed to pay for the engine.

For a week or more after the haystack fire there was no occasion to use the engine. It had been put in good shape by Cole, and parts of it had been given a fresh coat of paint, until it looked almost as good as new. Constable Stickler had practiced sending the signals, and the bell could be heard by the boys living in the farthest part of the town. As soon as members of the new fire department heard the signal they were to dress quickly, and hurry to Cole's barn. Thus, with the constable on the watch to detect the first sign of a blaze, the boys were ready to tackle the biggest kind of a conflagration.

One pleasant summer day, Bert and several of his chums were out in a rowboat on the lake. They frequently spent much time on the water, for there was good fishing in it and in the river which flowed into the lake, and they also had much fun swimming.

"Let's row over toward the big cove and have a dip," proposed Bert, who, with Tom Donnell, was at the oars. "It's getting too hot out here in the sun."

All agreed, and soon they were in a secluded part of the sheet of water. Big Cove, as it was locally called, was a sort of bay, almost out of sight from the main part of the lake. To reach it the boys had to row around a point, which extended for quite a distance out into the water. On this point was a boathouse, which was part of the property on which stood an old and what at one time had been a handsome residence. This was on a bluff, overlooking the lake, and was known as the Stockton mansion.

As the rowboat turned this point the boys were surprised to see a small motor craft shoot out from the boathouse.

"Look at that!" exclaimed Bert. "I didn't know there was one of those gasolene jiggers on the lake."

"Me either," added Tom. "Must be a new one. Wonder who's in it?"

"Must be somebody from the Stockton house," said Vincent; "though I didn't know anybody was living there now."

"Yes, there's somebody in it," added John Boll, "but I never knew they had a boat."

"Look out!" suddenly exclaimed Bert. "It's coming right for us!"

Sure enough the motor boat was headed straight for the

rowing craft, and it was coming on at top speed. No one could be seen in it, though the engine could be heard puffing.

"It's running away!" cried Tom. "Let's catch it!"

"Let's get out of the way, you mean," called Bert. "Do you want to be sunk in the deepest part of the lake? Pull on your left oar, Tom! Pull! Pull!"

The motor boat was now almost upon the other craft.

Frank V. Webster

CHAPTER IX

A NARROW ESCAPE

"Give a yell!" suggested Vincent.

"What for?" panted Bert, as he struggled with the oars, trying to swing the boat out of danger. "There's nobody aboard to steer the boat out of the way."

But Vincent yelled anyhow, and, to the surprise of the boys, a figure suddenly showed itself in the motor boat. It was that of a man, and he had been lying down in the craft, adjusting some of the machinery while the engine was running.

His sudden exclamation, as he sat up on hearing Vincent's yell, showed that he was not aware how close he was to a collision. He jumped to his feet, leaped forward to the wheel, and with a few quick turns sent his boat to one side.

And it was only just in time, for the freeboard of his craft grazed the extended oars that Tom and Bert had thrust out to dip in the water, in order to further swing their boat around.

"I didn't see you!" exclaimed the man, as his boat rushed past. "I was fixing my engine. I'm sorry!"

"Whose boat is that?" asked Bert.

But the man returned no answer, and in a few seconds he was

too far off to enable the boys to repeat the question.

"Do any of you fellows know him?" asked Bert of his chums.

"Seems to me I saw him in the village the other day," replied Tom. "He was buying some stuff in the drug store. He's a stranger in town."

"Wonder what he's doing around here?" asked Vincent. "It's a good thing I hollered when I did, or he'd have punched a hole in us."

"You're right," agreed Bert. "I didn't think there was anybody in the boat. But didn't he come out of the Stockton boathouse?"

"He sure did," replied Tom. "But there hasn't been a boat there in several years. We've been in swimming around here lots of times, and I never saw one before."

"Me either," chimed in several lads.

"And that's a new power boat," went on Bert. "It's a dandy, too. We ought to have a gasolene engine to work our fire apparatus."

"No, we shouldn't!" exclaimed Cole. "Those valves on our pumps wouldn't stand being worked too fast. Our engine is good enough as it is."

"Of course it is. We haven't had much use of it lately, have we?"

"No; but it's all ready when we get an alarm. I oiled her up good yesterday. And I guess the constable is on the job every night. He's as anxious for a fire as we are, for he wants to ring the bell."

"Still, I don't believe any one really wants a blaze," remarked

Bert, and then he added: "We can make another payment on the engine this week, and then we'll only owe twenty-six dollars."

"Oh, we'll soon have it paid for," declared Vincent.

By this time the boys had reached the "swimming hole," and, tying up their boat, they soon were undressed and splashing about in the water.

The lads had great fun, playing all sorts of games and tricks, but soon the descending sun warned them that it was time to start for home, and after a "last dive" they donned their garments and began rowing back around the point. They kept a watch for the motor boat, but saw nothing of it, nor did there appear to be any signs of life about the old mansion up on the bluff.

The Stockton house was a source of some mystery to the villagers. The mansion, which, years before, had been the scene of much life and gaiety, was owned by Harris Stockton, who was reputed to be quite wealthy. But one day he had disappeared, saying good-bye to no one, and it was generally supposed he had gone abroad, as he was rather eccentric, and given to going and coming most unexpectedly.

It was thought that the house was deserted, but neighbors frequently saw an old woman about it, after Mr. Stockton had disappeared, and she announced that she was the housekeeper, Sarah Blarcum by name. There was also a young man seen about the premises, and, in answer to questions from inquisitive persons, Mrs. Blarcum stated that the young man was Mr. Stockton's nephew, Alfred Muchmore, who was running the place during his uncle's absence. As to where Mr. Stockton had gone, Mrs. Blarcum did not know, though she said the nephew had given her to understand his uncle was traveling in Europe.

Muchmore was not known to any of the village people, and

seemed to keep pretty much to the mansion. He was seen about the grounds occasionally, but Mrs. Blarcum attended to all the marketing.

"Well, Herbert," said his mother that night, "you haven't had much use of your new engine, have you?"

"Not yet; but we will."

"Oh, I hope you don't have to go to any dangerous fires. I'm so afraid you'll get hurt."

"A fireman has to take chances, mother. Father had to do it, remember."

"But you are only a volunteer."

"That's the best kind. I think I'll get the boys together and have a practice run. We need a little drilling. But I'd just as soon an alarm wouldn't come in to-night. I'm dead tired, and I can sleep like a top, after my swim."

"Then if I hear an alarm from the church bell I suppose you don't want me to call you?"

"Of course, I do, mother. But I guess I'll hear the bell if it rings."

But Bert did not, and it was not until his mother had shaken him vigorously, several hours later, that he became aware of the frantic sounding of the fire alarm.

"Herbert! Herbert!" called his mother. "The fire bell is ringing!"

"Dong! Dong! Dong! Dong!"

The bell gave out four quick strokes. Then a pause.

"Dong! Dong! Dong! Dong!"

"It's on the west side of town!" exclaimed the boy, as he reached out and made a grab for his clothes. They were arranged on a chair near his bed, in readiness for quickly putting on; a practice observed by all the young members of the volunteer department.

"Look out of the window, mother, and see if you can discover a blaze, please," directed Bert, as he began to dress.

"Yes, I can see a light off in the west."

"That must be it. Did the bell ring long before you called me?"

"Only once. I was awake and heard it. Now, do be careful, Herbert. Don't get into danger." "I'll not, mother," and, with a kiss for his parent, Bert dashed down the stairs, and ran at top speed for Cole's barn. He saw several of his chums in the street, headed in the same direction.

CHAPTER X

MYSTERIOUS ACTIONS

"Where is it?" asked Bert, of Tom Donnell, whom he joined, almost as soon as he came out of the house.

"I don't know. I heard the four bells. Old Stickler is ringing yet. He didn't lose any time." "No, he didn't. Say, Vincent, do you know where it is?"

"I heard Simon Pierson say, as I ran past his house, a few minutes ago, that he thought it was the Stockton mansion. He can see it from his third floor."

"The Stockton mansion! If that gets going we can't put that out with our little engine."

"Maybe it's only a small blaze."

"I hope so," replied Bert. "But come on. We must run faster than this."

They found quite a crowd of the young firemen at Cole's barn when they got there. Cole had jumped out of bed at the first signal from the bell, and had lighted the lamps on the engine.

"Run her out!" he cried, as Bert and his chums came in sight.

"No, wait a few minutes," directed the captain. "We will need a few more fellows to haul her up the hill, and there's no use going off short-handed.

"But the fire will get too much of a start."

"Can't help it. Might as well not go at all as to go with not enough to work the engine. The bucket brigade would only laugh at us then."

"There's some of 'em now!" exclaimed Cole.

Out in the village street could be heard the tramp of running feet, and a man's voice crying:

"Come on, bucket brigade! We'll beat the new department!"

"Why don't the fellows hurry!" exclaimed Cole. "We'll get left!"

"Here they are!" shouted Tom Donnell, as about ten lads rushed into the barn. They lived on the far side of town, and had come in a bunch to respond to the alarm.

"Grab the rope, boys!" cried Bert. "Don't let the bucket brigade beat us!"

The long double line was run off the reel, and a two-score of ready hands grasped it. Cole, as was his privilege, jumped on the engine to steer, for he had rigged up a tiller wheel on it, since it had been in his barn, and this made it easier to pull, even with his added weight.

"Let her go!" he called, and with a rumble over the barn floor, the apparatus was hauled out, the bell on the engine clanging out a warning.

In the street in front of Cole's house, were several members of the bucket brigade, trying to catch up with the foremost men, who, under the leadership of Moses Sagger, were running toward the blaze.

These stragglers the young firemen shortly left behind, and soon they were almost up to the head of the line of the older fire-fighters.

"It's the Stockton mansion, all right!" cried Cole, as they got to the foot of the hill on which the big house stood. It could be plainly seen now, and flames were shooting from a side window.

"It hasn't got much of a start yet," shouted Bert. "Maybe we can put it out, boys, and save the house. Come on, for all you're worth!"

The lads needed no urging. They reached the burning house almost as soon as did the first contingent of the bucket brigade. Out in the yard was an old woman, wringing her hands, and crying:

"Oh, dear! Oh, dear! We'll all be burned up! The house will be destroyed! Oh, dear! Oh, dear!"

"Where is a well or cistern?" asked Bert, as he signalled his company to halt the engine.

"A cistern? Oh, dear! Here's one! But be careful you don't fall in. It's very deep. Oh, dear! This fire is terrible!"

The flames were gaining headway, but seemed to be only in one part of the house, on the east side.

"Run the engine close to the cistern," directed Bert. "Tom, you and John cut down the clothes line. Fasten some lengths to the buckets. We'll have to dip up the water from the cistern, and pour it into the engine tank. Vincent, you take charge here, and see to the buckets. Cole, get your fellows to the handles! Tom, you and Charlie Sanders take the nozzles! Lively now!"

Frank V. Webster

His orders were promptly executed. In a short time several buckets had long pieces of rope attached to them, by which they could be dropped down into the cistern, when the cover was removed. They could then be pulled up full, and the fluid emptied into the tank.

The hose was unreeled, and with the nozzles in charge of Tom and Charlie, Bert hurried into the house.

"Show us the way to where the fire is," he said to the old housekeeper.

"Right this way! Right this way!" she cried, hurrying into the side door of the house as fast as her tottering legs would carry her. "The fire's in an unused part of the mansion. It's near a chimney flue. Oh, dear! It's awful!"

Bert and his two chums followed her. Meanwhile, the bucket corps was rapidly dipping up water and filling the tank. The boys had not yet begun to work the handles, as Bert had arranged to give a signal, on a whistle he carried, when he wanted the water to begin to flow.

The tank was almost full, and Cole was beginning to wonder when the young captain would signal for the streams. The flames were becoming brighter and brighter, and were now shooting from windows on the side of the house, a big chimney, built up from outside, jutting out between the casements.

"Here, you boys git away from here, and let us git some water!" cried Moses Sagger, as, followed by several men he pushed his way to the cistern. He had been searching all about the premises for a well which the bucket brigade might use, but had not been successful.

"We were here first, and we're going to stay!" declared Vincent.

"That's what!" added Cole. "Besides, you men can't dip up any water unless you put some ropes on your buckets."

"Where are the ropes?" asked the butcher, as he saw the truth of that statement.

"You'll have to find 'em, same as we did," replied Vincent, as he and his chums continued to dip and fill. But the clothes line was all cut up, and there was no more rope in sight, save that by which the engine was hauled.

"Take that rope," suggested one member of the bucket brigade.

"Don't you dare touch that!" cried Cole. "Reel it up, boys, and if they try to take it, douse 'em with water."

"No, we haven't any right to take their rope," spoke a cooler-headed member of the men's fire department. "Come on to the lake, men. We've got enough men to make a long bucket line. There's plenty of water there."

Just then there came a blast from the whistle Bert carried.

"Pump!" yelled Cole. "Pump, boys!"

The lads, who had mounted to the top of the engine tank, began to work the handles with vigor, the flat hose bulged out, and, from the sound of the pumps, the young firemen knew they were sending out two vigorous streams.

"Now, boys, lively!" cried Vincent. "Give 'em all the water they can use!"

Thus it became a good-natured race between the two divisions of the department, one trying to pump as much water as possible, and the other seeing to it that the tank did not become empty. Because of the closeness of the engine to the cistern, and the fact that there was plenty of water in it, the tank was kept more than half full all the while.

Meanwhile, the bucket brigade had been formed, and was passing water from the lake. But, as it had to go, hand by hand in the buckets, up a flight of stairs, very little of the fluid reached the blaze. The fire had been gaining headway. Bert and his two chums had entered a long hall with their hose, and they saw where the floor and woodwork, adjoining the chimney, were on fire.

"Douse her out, boys!" cried Bert, as he signalled for the water. A moment later two big streams spurted from the brass nozzles, and fell with a hiss on the leaping flames.

"I'll take a look around and see if it's breaking out anywhere else," said Herbert. "One stream is almost enough there."

He turned aside, and started to run down another hall, that was at right angles to the one where the fire was. Suddenly a man confronted him, and, even in the excitement, Bert knew him for the individual who had been in the motor boat that nearly ran the boys down.

"Where are you going?" the man asked.

"To look and see if there is a blaze anywhere else," replied Bert.

"Who are you?" inquired the man, who appeared very much excited, more so than the occasion called for, since, as yet, the fire was not beyond control.

"I'm captain of the Boys' Volunteer Fire Department," replied Bert. "Who are you?"

"I'm Mr. Muchmore. I'm in possession of this house, and you can't pass here!"

"But I only want to see if there's another place on fire. We have two lines of hose, and one is enough back there."

"I don't care! You can't pass here!"

Bert wondered at the man's mysterious action, but the boy had no right to dispute the peremptory orders.

"Put out that fire back there," went on Mr. Muchmore, motioning to where Bert had come from. "That is all there is in the house. And don't you dare pass into this hall."

"Very well," replied the young captain, quietly, as he returned to Tom and Charlie.

Just then he thought he saw a flicker of flame beyond where Muchmore was standing. He started forward to investigate.

"Keep back, I tell you!" cried the man, and he thrust Bert to one side so violently that the young fireman hit the wall with considerable force.

"There's no need for you to do that!" Bert exclaimed, highly indignant. "I only want to help put out the fire!"

"You can't come in this hall!" declared the man, and then, before Bert could answer, he turned and ran along it at full speed.

"Well, he certainly acts queer," thought the boy, but, as a second look convinced him that there was no blaze in that part of the house, he returned to his chums.

In spite of their efforts the fire seemed to be gaining.

"See if they can't give us a bit more water!" cried Charlie.

Bert leaned out of a window, and whistled a signal that had been agreed upon, whenever more pressure was needed. The boys at the handles, who had lagged a bit, increased their strokes, and more water was available. A few seconds later Vincent, who had turned his supervision of the bucket corps over to John Boll, came into the smoke-filled hall.

"Can I help you, Bert?" he asked.

"Oh, yes!" exclaimed Mrs. Blarcum, the aged housekeeper, as she stood some distance back, out of the smoke. "There are some valuable paintings in that room, and they ought to be saved. Can you boys get them out?" and she pointed to the door of an apartment just back of where the two lads, with the hose nozzles, stood.

"Sure we will!" replied Vincent. "Come on, Bert. That will be easier than saving horses."

The flames seemed to be eating back, in spite of the efforts of the young firemen, and the aid given by the bucket brigade, which last was not much. They had run up ladders on the outside of the house, near where the flames were, and were throwing water on in that way.

"Why, the door's locked!" exclaimed Vincent, as he tried the knob. "Where's the key?"

"Locked!" repeated Mrs. Blarcum. "I didn't know that. The paintings will be burned, and Mr. Stockton was very fond of them. They cost a lot of money."

"We can break the door in!" cried Bert. "Come on, Vincent!"

The boys prepared to rush at the portal.

"Stop!" cried a ringing voice, and they looked up to see Muchmore hastening toward them. "Don't you dare go into that room!"

CHAPTER XI

SUSPICIONS AROUSED

For a moment the boys hardly knew what to do. They stood looking at Muchmore, who seemed very angry, and also intensely excited.

"We're going to save the pictures" said Vincent.

"There are no pictures in there!" declared the man.

"The housekeeper said so," put in Bert.

"Yes, yes! The valuable paintings belonging to Mr. Stockton!" exclaimed Mrs. Blarcum. "They'll be burned up! The fire is coming this way!"

"I don't care if it is!" fairly shouted Muchmore. "Let the pictures burn. As for you, old woman, if I find you meddling any more, with what doesn't concern you, I'll find a way to stop you! Now clear out!"

The woman shrank back, mumbling to herself, and hastened down the stairs.

"You boys are too fresh!" went on Muchmore. "Why don't you mind your own business?"

"Our business is to put out fires!" declared Herbert. "And

that's what we're doing here."

"Then keep out of places where you have no right to enter! There is no fire here!"

"But it may get here soon, and we wanted to save the things," added Vincent.

"Get out!" exclaimed Muchmore, in an angry voice. "Don't you attempt to go into that room. You'd better pay more attention to the blaze."

"The blaze is being attended to all right," replied Herbert. "We've got two streams on it. But if you don't want us to save any goods, I'm sure we don't mind. Come, Vincent, we'll leave."

The two boys, puzzled by Muchmore's queer actions, went back to where their companions were still playing water on the flames.

The fire was now under control, the boys having prevented its spread beyond a small area. Quite a hole was burned in the floor, and the flames had eaten through the side of the house, and burned out two windows. A little more water served to put out the last sparks.

"Guess we're done," said Charlie. "You can signal 'em to stop pumping, Captain Bert," and he laughed, for he was well pleased with his role of fireman. Bert blew the prearranged blasts on his whistle, and the boys at the brakes were glad enough to cease, for their arms ached with the strain. Those drawing water from the cistern likewise welcomed the respite.

"Take up the hose," ordered Herbert, with as much importance as if he was a battalion chief of a big city department.

Tom and Charlie went through the hall, dragging the two lines with them, and the hose was soon reeled back on the engine.

"Guess we've done our share," declared Mr. Sagger, as he called to his men of the bucket brigade. "The fire's out!"

"Well, I can't say that we did it all," Confessed Mr. Appelby. "The boys did the most of it."

"We could have done it without them," asserted the butcher. "They were only in the way. We couldn't use the cistern."

"I guess it's just as well they got there first," went on the mayor of Lakeville. "This looked like a bad blaze, and if it had got beyond control the whole house would have gone. It's as dry as tinder, and a regular death-trap."

"Did you hear what started it, Mr. Appelby?" asked Cole, as he trimmed the lamps on the engine.

"Overheated flue, according to the housekeeper. I was talking to her, but a young fellow came along and ordered her to stop. I wonder who he was?"

"That's Muchmore," declared Herbert "He's in charge since Mr. Stockton has been away. He didn't want us to do anything toward saving some pictures, and he kept me from going in a certain hall. He's a queer chap."

"I should say so," commented Mr. Appelby. "Maybe he lost his head on account of the fire."

"And he lost his manners, too," added Vincent, at the recollection of Muchmore's mean words.

"Well, the house is safe now," went on Mr. Appelby. "I guess we can leave. I suppose Muchmore can attend to things now. Let's gather up the buckets, Sagger, and go home. I'd like to get a little more sleep."

The bucket brigade soon left, and, a little while later, the young firemen, pulling their engine, moved off down the hill, talking over the events of the night. They all agreed that they had been more successful than might have been expected of a new organization.

"I think Muchmore might have at least thanked us," said Tom Donnell. "He didn't show up after his queer actions."

"There's something funny about that man," declared Bert. "I never saw a person act so suspiciously. He seemed afraid that we would discover something."

"Maybe he was," said George Perkins.

"What?" asked several of his companions.

"Why, I heard that he was a regular gambler," went on George. "He makes a profession of it. Maybe he had a gambling outfit in some of those rooms, and didn't want you to discover it."

"Who told you he was a gambler?" asked Vincent.

"The station agent. He sees him taking the train to the city every once in a while, and one day he saw him in a car, with a man he knows to be a gambler of the worst kind. Oh, Muchmore is a gambler, all right."

"Do you suppose he has gambling games in that house?" inquired Tom Donnell. "I shouldn't be surprised."

"I wonder if Mr. Stockton knows it?" ventured Bert. "I heard my mother say Mr. Stockton was a very fine man, and I don't believe he would allow that if he knew it."

"Nobody's liable to tell him," went on George. "He seems to have disappeared. That's another queer part of it. The station agent, who knows Mr. Stockton quite well, doesn't remember his going away, and he'd have to go from here to New York, if he sailed for Europe, which is the story Muchmore tells in the village."

"Boys," said Bert suddenly, "I believe there is something mysterious about that house. I thought so when I saw how queer Muchmore acted. Now, with what George tells me, I am more than ever inclined to that belief."

"What can we do about it?" asked Vincent.

"Maybe we can investigate," went on Herbert, "I'd like to find out more about the place."

"We might make an excuse for going there tomorrow, by asking if the fire did much damage," suggested Cole.

"And be put out for our pains," objected Vincent. "No, I'm going to stay away from there."

"I guess that will be best, for a time," decided Bert.

CHAPTER XII

SAGGER'S FIRE LOSS

Though the boys were not thanked by Muchmore, for their good work at the blaze in the Stockton mansion, the lads knew that they had done efficient service. Herbert, however, was not satisfied with his department.

"There are lots of things we'll have to do better," he told Vincent and Cole, the next day. "We get in each other's way, and we're not quick enough. Why, it took ten minutes for all of us to assemble last night."

"I don't see any other way of working it than the way we have been doing," replied Cole, "All the boys run when they hear the bell."

"Yes, I know, but the trouble is some of them have to run too far."

"How else can we do it?" asked Vincent.

"I've been thinking of a plan," replied the young captain.

"What is it?"

"Well, we might divide the company into three divisions. One division, say of about ten boys, could sleep in Cole's barn for two nights, or maybe three. Then, if an alarm came in they would be right there to rush the engine out. The other boys would stay in their homes, and, as soon as they heard the bell, they'd run to the fire. In that way they'd get to the blaze about the same time the engine would, and there'd be no delay."

"That is a good scheme," declared Cole. "We've got some old cot beds we could put here in the barn to sleep on."

"Oh, the hay's good enough in the summer time," replied Bert. "Of course, we couldn't stay here in the winter, unless we fixed up a place with a stove. Besides, in winter we have to go to school, and we haven't so much time to attend to fires."

"That's so, our department is liable to go all to pieces when school opens," admitted Cole. "That's too bad! And I was just thinking of a plan to attach my force pump to the engine, so as to give us three lines of hose."

"Say, haven't you got anything else to talk about except that force pump?" asked Vincent. "You must have it on the brain."

"Just the same, that's a dandy pump," went on Cole. "I put a new kind of valve in this morning, and she squirts a hundred feet now. Let me show you."

"No, let's talk some more about our department," said Vincent. "Do you think the boys will like this new plan, Bert?"

"I guess so. We'll ask 'em, anyhow. And then there's another thing."

"What is it?"

"I think we ought to have some drills. As it is now some of the boys don't know what to do. They don't pump good, and they don't pass water good. We ought to have more practice."

"So we had," admitted Vincent. "Lots of the fellows spilled about half the water on the ground last night, instead of putting it in the tank. They were so excited."

"A drill would help that," observed Bert. "We'll get the fellows together in a couple of nights, and talk things over."

This was done, and Bert's plan, of having a part of the force stay on duty in Cole's barn every night, met with instant approval. In fact they had to draw lots to see which boys would take the first three nights, as every one wanted that honor. It was arranged that those in the barn would rush out with the engine, as soon as they heard the alarm on the church bell. The others would assemble at the scene, as soon as they could get there. Some of the boys called it "camping out" to stay at the barn.

"And we'll have a drill to-morrow," said Bert. "We need lots of practice. There are some old buildings in this town, and if they get on fire we'll have a hard job putting them out."

"Especially if they're a good distance from water," added Cole.

The drill took place the next afternoon. A big fire, of old boxes, was built in a vacant lot, the location of which was known only to Bert and Vincent. At a certain time, the hour also being unknown to the boys, the bell was rung, permission to do so having been obtained.

One or two boys had been hanging around Cole's barn all day, having anticipated the alarm, and they wanted to rush off with the engine at once, but Vincent, who arrived shortly after the first round of two strokes, which showed that the fire was in the eastern section, would not permit this.

"No, we've got to wait for the others," he said. "It's only at night that the new plan is to go into effect."

Soon nearly every member of the company was at the barn, and, with yells, cheers and shouts, the boys dragged the engine through the streets to where the fire had been kindled.

"Pretty good!" exclaimed Herbert. "You got here in eight minutes, and it's farther than it was to the Stockton mansion. Now, then, douse the fire!"

The big pile of boxes was blazing furiously, but the boys ran the engine close to a small pond, the bucket corps got busy, the hose lines were unreeled, and, in less than three minutes, there was only a smoking heap where there had been fierce flames.

"That's the stuff, boys!" exclaimed Mayor Appelby, who was among the spectators that had gathered. "First thing you know the town will have to vote you an appropriation."

"Humph!" retorted Mr. Sagger, the miserly butcher. "If the bucket brigade was here we could do better than that. The brigade is good enough for Lakeville, and it keeps down taxes."

"Yes, and sends our fire losses up," added the mayor. "Insurance rates would be much lower if we had a good fire department, even as good a regular one as the boys' volunteer organization is."

"I don't believe it," declared the obstinate butcher.

For the next week the boys had several drills, and they showed a great improvement. The different divisions took turns sleeping in the barn, though they were disappointed that no alarm came in to test their abilities. Some improvements had been made to the engine, for Cole, after much experimenting, had mounted his force pump on the forward part of the tank, and attached a long garden hose to the spout. With it he could send a small stream a considerable distance, though not much water went through the small hose, as compared with the larger lines.

"It'll do for small fires," observed Cole, with much satisfaction, as he contemplated his work.

The very night that Cole finished the work of attaching his force pump, an alarm came in about eleven o'clock. The volunteer division, which was assigned to barn duty that night, had hardly retired to the cots or the haymow, when the clanging bell told them there was a blaze.

"Lively, boys!" cried Cole, who assumed the post of captain until Bert arrived.

Surely no boys ever dressed more rapidly than did the ten lads in the barn. In really quick time they were running the engine out of the driveway, and Cole cried:

"Three strokes! Over to the south side! Say! But it's quite a blaze, all right!"

The sky was already showing a bright glow.

"It's Sagger's butcher shop!" cried Tom Donnell. "Look, it's blazing like fury!"

The shop was indeed wrapped in flames.

"Fire! Fire! Fire!" cried Constable Stickler, and scores of voices joined in the shout.

"Come on! Come on!" yelled Mr. Sagger, as he stood in front of his store, fairly jumping up and down in his excitement. "The whole place will go if you don't hurry, boys!"

"I wonder why he doesn't shout for the bucket brigade now?" asked Cole, as he steered the engine as close as he could to the flaming structure.

"That's right, boys! Put out the fire!" cried Mr. Sagger. "I'll give you a hundred dollars if you save my shop!"

CHAPTER XIII

SINGING A DIFFERENT TUNE

From various directions came running the young members of the volunteer fire department. The bucket brigade was also on hand, and had formed a line from the town pump, which stood near the store, as close to the burning shop as they dared to go. The whole interior seemed a mass of flames.

"Where will we get water?" shouted Cole to Bert, who had arrived on the run.

"Back the engine down to the brook!" cried the young captain. "Isn't the hose long enough to reach from there?"

"Yep! Plenty!"

"Then back her down!"

The flames were crackling and roaring, and the smoke was so thick and choking, because of the burning meats and fats, that it was impossible to go very close. The bucket brigade had to beat a retreat, and, though they had the satisfaction of first getting water on the blaze, it was an empty honor.

"Lively, now, boys!" cried Bert. "Take one nozzle, Vincent! George, you grab another! Hold 'em here, and we'll unreel the hose when we back the engine!"

It was rather hard work to push the clumsy machine down through the yard of the house adjoining the butcher shop, to where the brook flowed back of the store. But it was accomplished by the boys unaided, for the men were busy trying to find some means of using their buckets.

"Dip and fill!" cried Bert, as the corps of pail handlers lined up from the engine to the brook.

Water began to splash into the tank and soon there was enough to begin pumping. Up and down went the long handles, impelled by the sturdy arms of ten boys.

"Wait!" cried Cole. "You're not using my force pump. Somebody take the hose. I'll work her!"

"I will!" cried Dick Harris, glad of the chance to handle a nozzle, even if it was only a small one, and unreeling the garden hose Cole had attached to his beloved pump, he started toward the burning butcher shop.

The young firemen soon found they had all they could do in quenching this fire. It was the fiercest one they had yet undertaken to subdue.

It was so hot that the boys at the nozzles had to be relieved every few minutes, and Bert was kept busy making shifts from the bucket corps or from among the pumpers.

The men's bucket brigade could only throw water on from the rear, where the fire was less hot, but the boys pluckily stuck to the front, and directed their three streams into the midst of the flames. Clouds of steam arose as the fluid fell on the hot embers.

"Can't you throw any more water on?" demanded Mr. Sagger, who continued to run up and down in front of his place, deploring his loss.

"We're doing the best we can," answered Bert.

"We ought to have a regular department, that's what we ought to have!" declared the butcher. "It's a shame that business men have to suffer losses by fire. What we need is a regular department here, with a steam fire engine."

"He's singing a different tune from what he did a week or so ago," thought Bert. "Then the bucket brigade was good enough. I guess he wishes we had two volunteer departments now."

It seemed as if the whole shop must go. The fire, as they learned later, had started in the sawdust packing of the ice box, and it had been smouldering for some time before being discovered. Then, with the sawdust and pine wood to feed on, in addition to the fat meats, the flames were more from what it had been at the Stockton blaze.

"Do you think you can save part of it?" asked the butcher, anxiously, of Bert. The man's manner toward the young fireman was quite different from what it had been at the Stockton.

"We're doing our best, Mr. Sagger," replied the young captain. "It's a hard fire to fight. The bucket brigade could come up closer now, the flames aren't quite so hot."

"That's so. I'll tell 'em." He ran to where the members of the department to which he belonged were futilely passing buckets of water.

"Why don't you come around front and closer?" the butcher asked them. "You ain't doing any good here!"

"Why don't you take a hand yourself?" demanded Silas Lampert. "You ain't doing anything but running up and down."

Frank V. Webster

"I'll help," declared Mr. Sagger. "I declare, I don't know what I am doing! This will be a heavy loss to me!"

"I guess you can stand it," murmured Mr. Lampert. "You got lots of money salted down, same as you have your pork."

"Come on, help me save the shop!" cried the butcher, and his fellow members of the bucket brigade followed him.

Fortunately, there was not much meat in the ice box, and when it had all been consumed, and there was only wood for the fire to feed on, the blaze was less fierce. The water from the three lines of hose and that dashed on by the men, who could now approach quite close, had its effect. In a little while the fire was about out, and Bert ordered the boys to use only one line of hose, which made it easier on the pumpers and bucket lads. Then, with a final hiss and splutter, the fire died away.

"It's a terrible loss!" declared the butcher, as he contemplated the ruins of his shop. "I'll lose over a thousand dollars."

"Haven't you any insurance?" asked Mr. Appelby.

"Yes, it's fully covered by insurance; but think of the trade I'll lose until I can build a new shop!"

"Oh, I guess you can put up some kind of a shack that will do for a while. We don't need much meat in the summer time."

"I tell you what it is!" exclaimed Mr. Sagger, "we've got to have a regular department, mayor; that's what we have! We can't have business places burn up this way. Why, it will ruin the town!"

"Well, if the taxpayers wanted a hired department they can have it," declared Mr. Appelby. "But it will cost money."

"Well, it ought to come out of the town treasury," went on the butcher. "Taxes is high enough now. Maybe we could get an engine cheap, somewhere."

"What's the matter with paying the boys for theirs ?" asked the mayor.

"No, we want men to run the department," objected the butcher.

"Those boys are as good as men," asserted Mr. Appelby, as he watched the lads, under Bert's direction, take up their hose and get the engine in shape for returning to quarters. "I guess old Sagger is afraid his taxes will go up. But we do need a regular department," he added to himself.

As Bert was getting the boys together to haul the engine back to the barn, he was approached by a man who emerged from the crowd.

"You did fine work," the man said, in a low voice.

Bert looked at him. It was the tramp stenographer he had pulled from the brook.

"How do you do!" the boy exclaimed. "How are you getting on?"

"First rate. I braced up after I met you. Guess that little bath did me good. I did some odd jobs for the farmers around here, and my health is better. Here's that quarter back."

"I don't want it."

"I suppose not; but I want to pay it. I've got a little money saved up, and the promise of a good job at my profession."

"Where?"

"Here in town. I'll tell you about it later, as I see you're busy," and, before Bert could ask any more questions, the tramp, whose appearance had improved considerably since the brook episode, was lost in the throng.

"That's queer," thought Bert. "I wonder who in this town would want a stenographer and typewriter?"

CHAPTER XIV

A DANGEROUS BLAZE

Somewhat puzzled over the words of the tramp, and vainly seeking a meaning for them, Bert turned to join his companions, who were hauling the engine away.

"Who was that fellow?" asked Vincent, who had noticed the man talking to his chum.

"Oh, a friend I once helped out of a difficulty," was the answer, and Bert smiled, as he described the brook as a "difficulty."

"What'd he want; more help?"

"No; he came to thank me. But, come on, let's hustle and get back to quarters. Wasn't it queer old Sagger's place should catch fire?"

"Yes. It serves him right, though, for all the mean things he's said about us."

"He's pretty mean, but I'm sorry his butcher shop is ruined."

"Oh, he's got money enough to build another."

The boys discussed the various scenes at the fire at some length, finally reaching Cole's barn, where the engine, after being cleaned and put in readiness for another alarm, was backed into place.

"I wonder if the town will take any action toward having a regular department now?" asked Vincent, as he and Bert walked toward their homes.

"They might. Sagger will make a big fuss over his loss, and, as he hopes to be the next mayor, he may start a movement. But I'm just as well satisfied to have the department the way it is, for a while. Of course, if the town took hold we could get another engine, and maybe a better alarm system. Constable Stickler can't always be depended on."

"Still, he's done pretty good."

"That's right. Well, so long, Vincent. See you to-morrow," and Bert turned down his street.

"So long," replied his chum. "Hope we don't get another alarm in to-night."

"I wonder who in this place can want a stenographer and typewriter?" again thought Herbert, as he went into the house. "I wish that tramp had told me. I meant to ask him his name, but I forgot all about it. Never mind, I may see him again."

There was considerable talk in Lakeville the day following the fire in the butcher shop. Most of it was done by Mr. Sagger himself, and the burden of his cry was that the town must have a regular department, with a big engine. It was pointed out to him that, without a water supply, a steam fire engine was out of the question, and then he said they ought to have another hand engine and some men to run both machines. He spoke of calling a meeting of the Selectmen to consider the matter, but nothing came of it. Probably Mr. Sagger figured up what it would cost, and feared his taxes would be too high. At any rate, nothing was done, though every time he mentioned the fire in his shop the butcher declared there ought to be a regular department. He never said anything about the hundred dollars he had offered for saving his shop.

Considering that the boys had worked hard at the Sagger blaze, Bert had no drills for a week. Then they were resumed again, and furnished plenty of exercise for the young firemen. But, about two weeks after the butcher shop fire, there came another which gave them almost more practice than they wanted.

It was shortly after midnight when the alarm came in, for Constable Stickler was an efficient guardian, in spite of his age, and on one of his trips to the church tower he had seen a flicker of flame off to the west. An instant later he was ringing the bell-four short, sharp, quick strokes.

The boys sleeping in the barn heard them, and so did the boys in their beds at home. They jumped up and, in quick time, the engine had been run out. It was Bert's night on "barn-watch," as it was called, and he and his chums hurried to such good effect that before the alarm had been rung four times they were pulling the engine from the barn.

"Whew! There's quite a wind!" exclaimed Bert as they got outside. "A fire to-night is liable to be a bad one."

"Hark! What's that?" inquired Cole.

The boys heard a distant shouting.

"The bucket brigade is turning out," spoke Tom Donnell.

"No. It's some one yelling about the fire!"

There came a shift in the wind, and to the ears of the boys was borne this cry:

"The lumber yard's on fire! Hurry!"

Frank V. Webster

"The lumber yard!" exclaimed Captain Bert. "If that gets going we can't do anything to stop it!"

"We've got to try," declared Cole.

"Of course," answered Bert, as if any one doubted it. "Come on!"

They increased their pace, and as they neared the end of the long street, they were joined by several of their comrades, who had rushed from their houses half-dressed.

"Where's the fire?" called Bob Fenton, who was hardly awake yet.

"Bergman's lumber yard, I heard some one yell," answered Bert. "And this wind blowing right across the lake toward it!"

The lumber yard of Perrett Bergman was located on the edge of the lake, where boats could easily unload their cargo of timber. It was quite a large yard, and was one of the principal industries of Lakeville. As Bert had said, the wind was blowing right across the lake. The breeze was a stiff one, and if it was sending the flames in among the pile of dried and seasoned boards the fire was likely to be a furious one.

But the boys did not falter. They dragged their rumbling engine as fast as they could, the bell clanging loudly as Cole pulled the cord attached to it. The little company was constantly being increased in numbers. Many of the young firemen, however, had proceeded directly to the scene of the conflagration.

The lurid light in the sky seemed to grow brighter, and there was a thick pall of smoke visible now.

"It's getting worse!" cried Cole.

"You don't expect it's going to put itself out, do you?" asked

Frank Burton. "Wait till we get there!"

A little later they turned into the street leading to the lumber yard. As they did so the blaze shone full in their faces, and they saw where the fire had originated. One of the big lumber barges that plied on the lake was on fire at the dock, and the flames were blowing right toward the heart of the yard, with its piles of timber.

"We've got our work cut out for us!" cried Bert.

"We'll have plenty of water, anyhow," shouted back Cole. "My force pump can be used, too!"

"He'd say something about his force pump if we had a steam fire engine," murmured Vincent.

"Run her right down, boys," called Bert. "Get as close to the water as you can!"

The boys picked their way through the piles of lumber. Already several members of the town bucket brigade were on hand, and they were standing in the shallow part of the lake, dipping up water in their pails and dashing the fluid on the blazing barge. "Volunteers this way!" sung out Bert, and several of his chums, who were already on hand and waiting, hastened to join their comrades.

But now a new problem was presented. The flames, eating their way among the dry lumber on the barge, had assumed a fierceness that made it impossible to run the engine down on the dock. In fact, the pier was already ablaze in places. Great glowing embers were being carried by the wind into the middle of the yard, but this danger had been seen, and several men were putting out the big sparks as fast as they fell.

But there was every chance that several tiers of lumber near the wharf would ignite from the flames sweeping from the barge. If one or two piles caught, the whole yard would go.

"What are we going to do?" cried Vincent to the young captain. "We can't get out engine down there!"

Bert was puzzled. It was a new problem for the amateur fireman, and he hardly knew what to do. But to get close enough to the blaze to use the engine and at the same time have a supply of water, was not an easy thing to work out.

Just then the burning barge swung down the lake, for the cables had been eaten through by the flames, and the wind was carrying it away. The sight of that gave Bert an inspiration.

"Come on!" he cried. "I see a way!"

"How?" asked Cole.

"We'll run the engine out on that empty flat-boat. We can pole it out into the lake, and play on the barge from the side where there are no flames! Lively, now, boys!"

They saw his meaning at once. There were plenty of boards at hand to make a runway for the engine, and in a little while it was on the flatboat. Then, with long poles which reached to the bottom of the lake, the boat was shoved out from shore.

"The barge is adrift!" cried Tom Donnell.

"Then we've got to go after it!" responded Bert. "We can make a line fast and tow it away, or it will set the other barges below here on fire, and we'll have more than we can handle. If we can keep the blaze to the one barge we'll be all right"

It was hard work, but the boys accomplished it. They put their flatboat close to the side of the blazing craft, where there were no flames, and made fast. Then they poled both boats well out into the lake.

"The dock is burning!" cried Cole.

"Let the bucket brigade attend to that," answered Herbert. "We've got our hands full here!"

Indeed they had, but the contest was more even now. The boys, using buckets with ropes attached, dipped from the lake the water which they poured into the engine, tank, and then the three streams were turned on the burning barge.

CHAPTER XV

A GENEROUS OFFER

Never since they had organized their little department had the boys worked under such difficulties. There was no getting away from this blaze. They were fast to it, and to cut loose meant to endanger other lumber barges nearby, which would mean a terrible conflagration.

It was hard work to keep the burning boat and that on which the engine was out in the lake, as a strong wind was forcing them both toward shore. It was also difficult to operate the pump, for the engine did not set level, and the boys on top of the tank had to cling there as best they could and send the big handles up and down. It was hard work to stand the fierce heat and choking smoke which enveloped them every now and again, as the wind shifted.

But the boys were no "milksops." They stuck to it, though it meant much physical pain. They gritted their teeth, and held their breaths when it was necessary. Some clung to the poles like grim death and prevented the barges from drifting, and all the while others were dipping and pumping water.

"I—I think we've got her!" cried Cole, when this desperate work had been going on for ten minutes.

"Don't be too sure!" cautioned Captain Bert. "There's lots of fire yet!"

There was, but the three streams of water, even if one was a small one, were beginning to tell. Gradually the flames amid the lumber on the barge began to die away. Once or twice it seemed as if the boat would break loose and go drifting down on the others, but grit told, and the boys held the craft.

"She's out now!" cried Vincent, as only a pall of smoke seemed to hang over the barge, and the boys at the brakes, hearing this with feelings of relief, ceased pumping. No sooner had they stopped than the flames burst out in a new place, and flared up fiercely.

"Jump right on the barge and take the hose with you," cried Bert, for the fire had been extinguished on that end of the barge nearest the flat-boat. "The water will do more good at close range."

The young firemen needed no second order. Dragging three lines of hose with them they leaped aboard the flaming boat and scrambled over the piles of charred lumber to the farther end, where the flames now were.

Then the fire gave up the fight. The last flame was quenched and the boys could take a much-needed rest.

"What'll we do now?" asked Cole of Bert. Every one seemed to depend on the young captain for instructions.

"I think we'd better run the barge ashore below here," he said. "Then there'll be no danger if the fire breaks out again."

"I'll guarantee that fire won't break out again," boasted Cole. "We soaked it too well."

"You can't tell what a fire will do," replied Bert. "It may be smouldering down in a corner where the water didn't reach."

"Have Cole leave his force pump on guard," suggested

Vincent, "That pump ought to be able to put out a fire all alone."

"Humph! That pump's all right, if you do make fun of it!" declared the owner of the latest addition to the fire apparatus. "It'll throw a stream farther than either of the big hose on this engine."

"Well, let's run the barge ashore, then pole back and get our engine off," proposed Bert. "I guess it's safe enough to leave the barge now."

They tied the blackened load of lumber in a little shallow cove, where, if it did start to burn again, no damage would result. Then they went back to the lumber yard, where they found a big crowd waiting them. The fire on the dock had been extinguished by members of the bucket brigade and had not amounted to much.

"Boys, I want to shake hands with every one of you!" exclaimed a voice, as Bert led his command ashore. "You did me a great service to-night, and I'll not forget it. But for your prompt action my lumber yard would have been destroyed and several of my valuable barges besides."

The speaker was Mr. Perrett Bergman, owner of the lumber yard, and, as each boy stepped ashore, he shook him warmly by the hand.

"Yes, Mr. Bergman, those boys certainly did themselves proud," said Mayor Appelby. "They're almost as good as a regular department."

"That's what they are. Well, I'll have something to say about that later. Now, I must go and see if there are any stray sparks around anywhere, and I want to investigate this fire. I have an idea it was set by tramps. That barge came down the lake early this evening, and the men in charge of it told me they threw a tramp overboard who was stealing a ride on it."

"Threw him overboard?" repeated Mr. Appelby.

"Yes. I told them that was the wrong thing to do, as the man might have been drowned, but lumbermen are rather rough. However, the tramp swam ashore, they told me. I have an idea he might have set the barge afire for revenge."

"It's possible," admitted the mayor. "I'll tell Constable Stickler to be on the watch for any suspicious characters."

Bert, who heard this conversation, wondered if the tramp he had rescued from the brook, or any of his companions, had started the fire.

"I hope the one I saved didn't do it," mused the boy. "He seemed like a decent chap in hard luck." Nothing was ever learned, however, of how the fire started. Certainly the tramp stenographer had nothing to do with it.

Several members of the bucket brigade assisted the boys in getting the engine off the flatboat. In fact, of late the men fire-fighters of Lakeville were beginning to entertain different feelings toward their boy rivals. They saw that the lads meant business, and that they were a corps of very efficient young-sters. Some of the men imagined that the volunteers were only doing the thing for fun, but what happened at the lumber yard blaze convinced them that they were mistaken.

"We seem to be right in it," remarked Cole, as they were dragging the engine back to quarters a little later. "Plenty of fires for us to put out lately."

"Yes. I wonder what Mr. Bergman meant when he said he'd not forget what we did for him?" asked Vincent.

"Oh, probably he's just like old Sagger," replied Tom Donnell. "You remember, Sagger promised us a hundred dollars for helping put out the fire in his shop."

"That's so; he did."

"Yes, but we haven't seen the hundred dollars yet, and I don't believe we ever will," declared Tom. "He's too stingy to give it to us. If we had it we could finish paying for the engine and get uniforms. That's what we need. I've worn out two suits of clothes running to fires lately."

"Uniforms would be a good thing to have," admitted Bert. "We need rubber boots, especially. My feet are soaking wet. It doesn't matter so much in summer, but if we go to a fire in the winter and get wet through it won't be so nice."

"Well, I don't believe Mr. Bergman will ever do anything for us," insisted Tom.

But he was mistaken. The very next day Bert received a letter from the owner of the lumber yard, in which Mr. Bergman thanked the young firemen for what they had done. Nor was this all. Enclosed in the letter was a check for two hundred dollars.

"I send you this as a small taken of my appreciation," the letter read. "Not that it pays for the work you did, for you saved me a good many hundred dollars by pulling that barge out of the way. But this is only a starter. I understand your engine is not yet paid for, and that you have no uniforms. Please use the check for that purpose. You will also hear further from me in a few days. I have a plan to propose, but I want to talk it over with the town authorities first."

"Say, he's all right!" exclaimed Cole, when Bert showed him the letter and check.

"He certainly is. I was barking up the wrong tree," admitted Tom. "Say, we'll be a sporty department, all right! Let's get red and blue uniforms. They'll look swell!"

"I wonder what his plan is?" asked Bert. "He says he has to

consult with the town authorities about it."

"Maybe he wants us to take in the bucket brigade," ventured Vincent.

"Better wait and see," advised Bert.

CHAPTER XVI

MR. BERGMAN'S PLAN

Never had Lakeville been so stirred as when, a few days after the lumber yard fire, notices were posted in various parts of the town, stating that a special meeting of the Selectmen would be held to take action on an offer made by Mr. Bergman to equip a regular fire department for the place.

"So, that's what he meant!" remarked Bert, when he read the notices. "Well, I wonder where we'll be, if they have a regular department?"

"Oh, I suppose the bucket brigade will be taken in, and they'll run the whole thing," said Vincent, a little bitterly.

"If they do, we'll keep our old hand engine and run to blazes just the same," declared Cole.

"That's what we will," added Captain Bert.

The notices announced that the meeting would be a public one, and would be held in the town hall, over the post-office. Opportunity would be given for all interested to state their views, the notice added.

"Then we'll state ours," threatened Cole. "Bert, can't you go there and make a speech?"

"I suppose I can, if the boys want me to. But what shall I say?"

"Oh, wait until we get there and see how things look. But if they want to turn us down, you get up and protest. We'll stand by you."

"All right," agreed Bert. "I think we ought to have something to say."

"So do I," came from Tom Donnell. "Put it good and strong, Bert."

The night of the meeting found nearly every male resident of Lakeville present, and there were some women and girls in the audience. In the meanwhile, the members of the volunteer department had used Mr. Bergman's donation to pay off the small balance due on their engine, and had purchased their uniforms. They were quite natty, consisting of blue trousers and red shirts, with helmets of the same fiery color, and belts with a large brass buckle in front.

The boys marched into the hall in a body, and took seats together.

"Oh, aren't they just too cute for anything!" exclaimed Nellie Travers to her chum, Jane Alton.

"They look quite business-like," commented Jane.

"Yes, but those uniforms are dear, aren't they?" "I don't know. I heard my brother Ned say they were quite cheap," went on Jane, who was something of a joker.

"Oh, Jane! You know I mean they're too sweet for anything! I just wish there'd be a fire alarm come in now, so I could see them run."

"I don't; I want to see what they're going to do at this meeting. Ned is worried for fear they'll break up the boys' department."

"That would be a shame."

"I think so, too. But, hush! Mayor Appelby is going to speak."

The mayor, who had been elected chairman of the meeting, told the object of the gathering. He said they had assembled to hear an offer that was to be made by their "distinguished fellow citizen, the Honorable Perrett Bergman." There were some cheers and applause at this, and Mr. Bergman arose.

"What I have to say will not take up much of your time," he began. "You all know we have had several fires lately, and that a number of lads of this village have constituted themselves a fire department. I need not point out what good work they have done. It speaks for itself.

"The recent blaze in my lumber yard has confirmed an impression I have had for some time, and that is, that we should have a regular department in this village. I think, with all due respect to it, that we have outgrown the bucket brigade!"

"That's right!" called some one from the rear of the hall.

"The bucket brigade did good work," asserted Moses Sagger.

"I know that," admitted Mr. Bergman, "but the village is growing. I do not hesitate to say that if it had not been for the boys' volunteer department I would be a much poorer man to-night than I am."

"Hurrah for the boys!" exclaimed a man, and there were hearty cheers.

"In brief, my offer is this," continued Mr. Bergman. "I am willing to buy a complete outfit for a fire department. I will furnish everything except the members of it, and I will even pay for having installed an electric alarm system, with pull boxes in various places. I will also equip a small fire headquarters. In view of the fact that we have no water system,

I would suggest that chemical engines be used."

"That's right," came from Mayor Appelby.

"I now, then, offer to purchase two of the best chemical engines that can be bought," went on Mr. Bergman. "I think we will not need horses, as the engines are light, and half a dozen persons can haul them. With two of these machines, one on either side of the town, we can take care of almost any ordinary blaze, as the houses here are not so close together that we will have any great conflagration. Now it remains for the town to act on my offer. Remember, I will furnish all the money needed for the engines, and to fit up a headquarters. All I ask the town to do is to supply the members and places in which to keep the engines."

"You have heard the very generous offer of our distinguished fellow townsman and public-spirited citizen, the Honorable Perrett Bergman," said Mayor Appelby, pompously. "What have you to say?"

"I say take it!" exclaimed Moses Sagger, quickly. He saw a chance for a good fire department without any increase in the taxes.

"That's right! Accept the offer!" came from various parts of the hall.

"With thanks!" added a more thoughtful man.

"You seem to be of one mind," went on the mayor. "I shall now put the question to a vote."

"One moment, if you please," began Bert, rising to his feet. He was rather pale, for he was not used to speaking in public.

"What is it, Herbert?" asked Mr. Appelby. "Don't you favor this?"

"I most certainly do, and so do all the boys. All we want to know is, what will become of our department?"

"Oh, we won't need you boys when we get the chemical engines," said Mr. Sagger quickly. "The members of the bucket brigade will attend to them. You boys can give your old engine away if you want to."

"We'll do nothing of the kind!" exclaimed Bert. "We bought and paid for that engine, when there was no prospect of Lakeville having anything like a department. Now we have a good organization and—"

"Yes, and we can put out fires!" interrupted Cole. "My force pump—"

"Dry up!" exclaimed Vincent, pulling Cole by the coat-tails. "Let Bert do the talking."

"That's all right. I was going to tell them about my force pump," murmured Cole.

"They don't want to hear it. Listen."

"I think we ought at least be allowed to continue our organization, and be recognized by the town as a part of the fire department," went on Bert. "We don't ask to run your chemical engines, but we would like to keep our hand engine."

"No, we don't want it!" cried Mr. Sagger. "We have no use for you boys. The men can run things in this town, We'll merge the bucket brigade into a regular department."

"That's what we will!" came from some of the older members of that ancient organization. "Then we might as well go home, boys!" exclaimed Herbert, somewhat bitterly. "They have no use for us here."

"One moment!" exclaimed Mr. Bergman, rising in his seat.

Everyone turned to look at him.

"I think some of you men are under a little misunderstanding," he went on. "My offer to buy two chemical engines was made because of the very efficient work the boys of this town did in putting out the fire in my lumber yard. I most certainly will not consent to thrusting the boys aside, now that we are about to have a regular department."

"Hurrah!" came from the irrepressible Cole. "My force pump—"

But his companions made him keep silent.

"I may say," went on Mr. Bergman, with a look at the boys, in their natty uniforms, "that my offer depends on one thing."

"What is that?" asked Mr. Appelby quickly.

"It is this: That the boys are to be in charge of the regular department, just as they now are of the volunteer one!"

"Hurrah!" cried Cole again, and his chums joined in with him. "My force—"

"Ain't the bucket brigade going to run things?" inquired Mr. Sagger.

"With all due respect to that organization, they are not!" replied Mr. Bergman loudly. "I will furnish the money for the engines only on the condition that the same boys, who did such good work at the fire in my place, continue in charge. The members of the bucket brigade may join if they wish, but the boys are the ones I want to see in control. They have proved what they can do, and I would recommend that Captain Herbert Dare be made the chief of the new department!"

"Whoop!" shouted Cole, standing up, and waving his hat. "That's the stuff! Whoop! Hurrah!"

CHAPTER XVII

THE ENGINES ARRIVE

There was instant excitement in the hall. Everyone seemed to be talking at once. The boys of the town were standing together, cheering for Herbert. Mayor Appelby was vainly rapping for order. At last Mr. Sagger made his voice heard above the others.

"I say if that boy is made head of the fire department none of us men will join!" he shouted. "We'll stick to the bucket brigade!"

"That's what!" declared several of his cronies.

"I wish you to remember one thing," replied Mr. Bergman. "I am paying for this improvement, and I think I ought to have something to say about it. Another thing, the town ought to be glad to get a good, up-to-date department. If you don't accent my offer then I must consider moving my lumber yard to a location where there is better fire protection."

This was something of which no one had thought, A number of the men of Lakeville found employment in the lumber yard, and if it went to some other town it would mean quite a loss.

"Then there is one last point," went on Mr. Bergman. "These boys know more about fighting fires than you men ever will. They have showed that already, and I want to give them due credit. I think Herbert Dare has proved that he knows how to handle a blaze, and how to use his force of boys to the best advantage. I have learned that his father was a regular city fireman. Either he is to be made chief of the new department or there isn't going to be any department."

This was plain talk, and the objectors knew Mr. Bergman meant it.

"I, for one, would be only too glad to see the boys run the department," said Mayor Appelby. "They have more time than we have."

"That's so," agreed a number, as the sentiment began to swing around the other way.

"I'd like to say a few words," spoke up Herbert, rising in his seat.

"Go on!" invited Mr. Appelby encouragingly.

"This offer of Mr. Bergman's is a complete surprise to me," said the boy. "I never sought the position of head of the new department."

"We know that," spoke a friendly voice.

"And I want to say that if there is going to be any feeling over the matter I'd rather not have it," went on Bert. "We boys will continue our own department and—"

"You'll do nothing of the kind," interrupted Mr. Bergman. "Lakeville is going to take a step forward, and you boys are the best persons to help her."

"I don't want to take the place, and feel that there is jealousy," added Herbert. "I admit I would feel proud of the honor, but—"

"He's the best chief we could have," interjected Cole, "and with my force pump—"

"That'll do you," put in Vincent, pulling Cole back to his seat for the seventh time.

"Let's vote on it!" called a man. "I'm in favor of the boys every time! Remember, they'll be men in a few years."

This brought matters to a head. There was considerable more discussion, but, with the exception of two or three, everyone was in favor of Mr. Bergman's plan, for he had used arguments that appealed to the majority.

A vote was taken, and was almost unanimous in favor of accepting the offer, and putting the boys in charge, with Herbert Dare as chief. As there were to be two engines, Vincent Templer was made assistant chief, to be in charge of the second apparatus.

Other officers were named from among the boys, and, as there were to be two companies, located in different parts of the town, places were made for all the lads who cared to join.

It was decided to keep the old hand engine for use in emergencies, and, as there would be no need of any one operating the new engines, since they worked automatically, the young fire fighters were advised by Mr. Bergman to develop themselves into a sort of salvage corps, to save goods at a fire, while one or two boys were at the chemical nozzles.

This much being accomplished, Mr. Bergman went into financial details with the officials of Lakeville. It was decided to have a simple alarm system, with boxes located at the more prominent places in the village, and an arrangement whereby the signal would be sounded on a big bell, which would be erected on a steel tower.

It took some time to put these improvements into shape, but

in about three weeks they were finished, and the two chemical engines had arrived from the factory.

"Say! They're beauties!" exclaimed Cole, happily, as he and the other boys went down to the freight depot to see them. "I wonder if they can throw a stream as far as my force pump?"

"Are you still talking about your force pump?" asked Tom Donnell.

"Well, it's a good pump," replied Cole, defending his invention.

"Wait until you see these," said Mr. Bergman, who had come to superintend unloading the engines.

Each chemical apparatus consisted of a large copper tank on four wheels. It had a long hose, on a reel, and a rope to pull the machine by, similar to the old hand engine.

But the principle of the new engines was entirely different. They shot a chemical stream at the fire, instead of one of merely water, and carbonous acid, or, as it is commonly called, carbonic acid gas, was generated. Fire will not burn where this gas exists, so that a small stream of the chemical was more effective than a big stream of water. The gas, being heavier than air, forms a sort of blanket over a blaze.

In the big copper tank was placed water, in which was dissolved some bicarbonate of soda, the sort mothers use to cook with. Then, in a small receptacle, fitting in one end of the big cylinder, was some sulphuric acid, or oil of vitriol. The two liquids were prevented from mixing until the proper time, by a simple arrangement.

When a fire occurred the chemical engine was to be hurried to the place. The hose would be unreeled, and then a lever and valve wheel would be turned, breaking the glass receptacle in which the sulphuric acid was held. This allowed the acid to

Frank V. Webster

mingle with the solution of soda water, and a strong gas was at once formed. The gas was under such pressure that it forced the combined soda and acid solution out through the hose for a considerable distance. It could be played on the fire, the gas would be generated, and the blaze would be extinguished in much less time than if water was used, and there would be less damage done.

"Those are certainly fine engines," declared Bert. "I guess we'll have to have some practice with them before we'll know how to run them."

"They are very simple in operation," said Mr. Bergman. "We'll arrange for some tests soon."

"We ought to have a parade," suggested Vincent. "Let's take 'em through the town, and show the people what we've got."

"A good idea," declared Mr. Bergman. "And, while we're about it, why not have a picnic."

"A picnic?" repeated Bert.

"Yes. Why not? Every village fire department has a picnic once a year. I don't see why Lakeville can't. It will stir the people up, and get rid of some of this jealous feeling."

"I guess the boys would like it all right," replied Bert.

"Then we'll have it over in Tillman's grove. I'll make the arrangements, and let you boys know when it's to be. Now we'd better get the engines into quarters."

It had been decided to keep one engine in Cole's barn, and another in the basement of the town hall, as these two places were far enough apart to give good protection in case of fire. The alarm system had been installed some days before, and Lakeville was now in good shape to take care of a blaze. Several members of the bucket brigade made application to join the new department, and they were taken in. Moses Sagger and some of his cronies, however, still held out.

As the boys dragged the new chemical engines through the town, quite a crowd came out to look at them. The machines glittered with brass and copper, highly polished, and made a fine appearance.

"Them things don't look as if they could put out a fire," said an old resident, who was used to seeing the bucket brigade or a hand engine at work. "Why, there ain't no pump, nor yet any pails."

"They say the pump's inside that there big copper cylinder," explained a man standing near him.

"Humph! Looks like an old wash boiler stuck on four wheels. That ain't any good. You need water to put out a fire."

"You do, eh?" thought Cole, who overheard this remark. "Well, we'll show you, some day."

The engines were soon in their quarters, and were charged with the soda and acid, according to the directions sent by the manufacturers.

"Now, we're all ready for a fire!" exclaimed Bert, as he and his chums looked at the machine in Cole's barn, while an equally admiring throng had gathered at the town hall, where Vincent was to be in command.

"I wish we'd get a big fire now," said one small lad, as he patted the big copper cylinder.

"Hold on, little man!" exclaimed Mr. Bergman. "We didn't get the engines for that. I haven't gotten over the scare about my lumber yard yet. Wait a bit, before you wish for a fire."

"I—I meant a bon-fire." replied the little fellow.

"Oh—that! Well, maybe we'll have one at the picnic."

CHAPTER XVIII

THE PARADE AND PICNIC

Announcement was made next day, by Mr. Bergman, that the new fire department, of which he was considered the patron, would have a grand parade and picnic in about a week. Members of the fire fighting organizations of neighboring towns were to be asked to take part, and there would be competitive drills, sports and games.

The people of Lakeville hardly knew what to think. So many things had taken place in the last few months that the town seemed like a person awaking from a long sleep, and finding himself in a new place.

"Lakeville is certainly improving," remarked Mr. Appelby to a group of men in the post-office one day, as they were reading the notice about the parade and picnic.

"That's what it is," added Mr. Charles Daven, the aged postmaster and a justice of the peace. "Why there's been more mail come to this here office in the last two weeks than in two months afore."

"How do you account for that?" asked Mr. Appelby.

"Why nearly every resident has written to some friend, tellin' of the new engines an' fire department, an' the pussons has writ back, askin' how we done it. I know, 'cause lots of 'em writ on postal cards, an' I read 'em. I read all th' postals you know," he went on, as if that was his privilege, "only now there's gittin' to be so much mail, I don't half finish with 'em, 'fore some pusson comes in an' takes 'em away. But business is certainly improvin' wonderful."

"And the taxes will go up likewise," added Mr. Sagger with a scowl.

"Not on account of the fire department," declared the mayor. "That hasn't cost the town a cent. Mr. Bergman footed the bills."

"But it will in time. He ain't going to live forever."

"Well, the town ought to be glad to pay 'em in a few years. More folks will come to live here if we have good protection from fire, and if the village gets bigger the taxes will be less."

"Well, I ain't going to pay any more," declared the miserly butcher.

Preparations for the picnic went on rapidly. Tillman's grove was on the edge of the lake, about three miles from Lakeville, and social gatherings were frequently held there in the summer time.

It was planned that the new fire department would parade through the town, hauling the chemical engines with them, go out to the grounds and there take part in a competitive drill which Mr. Bergman had arranged with the assistance of Bert and Vincent, and the chiefs of some nearby departments.

In order that there would be protection to Lakeville, in case a fire should occur during the picnic, Constable Stickler was to be left on guard part of the day, and a man would relieve him at a certain hour, so that the old official might see part of the fun. In case of a fire, a messenger was to be dispatched on horseback, to summon the department.

It was also planned to have the old hand engine in the parade, some of the smaller boys begging for the privilege of hauling this, a request which was quickly granted by Bert and his chums.

"Going to parade, Moses?" asked Mr. Appelby of the butcher, the evening before the day of the picnic.

"Parade? Not much! I wouldn't be seen with them whipper-snappers of boys."

"Well, those boys are all right, let me tell you. If it hadn't been for Herbert Dare and his crowd, Lakeville wouldn't have a fine fire department to-day, and your shop would be down to the ground. And another thing, insurance is less. I renewed mine to-day, and the agent said he could give me a lower rate, as the risk of loss from fire was less now that we had two good chemical engines."

"If we had enlarged the bucket brigade it would have done just as well, and saved a lot of money," declared the butcher.

"Oh, nonsense. You're an old fossil, Moses. Why Lakeville amounts to something to-day. Jamesville folks can't laugh at us any longer for not having an engine. I'm proud to live in Lakeville, and I didn't use to be. Guess I'll run for mayor again."

"I thought you said you wasn't going to," said Mr. Sagger quickly, as he knew he was pretty sure of the nomination, if the genial Mr. Appelby, whom everyone liked, did not enter the contest.

"Well, I've changed my mind. It's an honor to be mayor of a town with a good fire department."

Mr. Sagger said nothing, but he thought much.

No one could have wished for a better day than that of the

parade and picnic. It was a trifle warm, but it would be cool in the grove near the lake. The boys were up early, attired in their new uniforms, and after an early breakfast headed for one or the other of the two engine quarters.

The two machines were polished so one could see his face in them. There had been but one fire since they arrived, and that was a small one in an old shed. The engine in Cole's barn had been used to put out the blaze, and the quick manner in which it accomplished the task showed the boys of what sort of work the chemical was capable.

The other machine was as untried as the day it came off the train, but it was known to be in good working order. It was planned to have a drill between the two Lakeville companies, to see which could quickest get to a fire from a certain spot, and the one which won in that contest, would enter another in which would compete the departments from Jamesville, Weedsport and Northville Centre. A prize of a silver trumpet had been offered by Mr. Bergman for the company doing the best and quickest work.

At last all was in readiness for the parade. Mr. Bergman had engaged a band, and, to the thrilling strains of a lively march, the two chemical companies, with their machines, and the younger boys, in charge of the old hand engine, stepped out, and began a tour of the town.

How proud the lads were in their gay uniforms! It was the first time they had all been together, and the bright sunshine illuminating their ranks, and reflecting from the polished surfaces of the engines, made a picturesque scene.

Herbert Dare led his company in front, and behind him came fifteen boys, dragging on the long rope. In the rear of the engine came five other lads, armed with axes and long hooks, which were part of the new equipment.

In the second division was Vincent and his company, while at the rear brought up the smaller boys with the hand engine. Altogether it made a fine showing for Lakeville.

After marching through the principal streets of the town, and being admired by the throngs that gathered, the young firemen set off for the picnic ground. Thither, also, went most of the inhabitants of Lakeville, for it was a chance that might never come again, and everyone who could, took advantage of it.

"Whew! But it's hot!" exclaimed Cole, who was marching along beside Bert, no particular formation being maintained on the road to the grounds.

"You'll be cooler pretty soon," consoled the young chief. "I wonder if we can beat those fellows?" he added, referring to the members of the other fire companies.

"I'm not afraid of the Northville Centre bunch," declared Cole, "but Jamesville is a different proposition. The chief there is a hustler, and I understand they are pretty quick. They've had lots of practice."

"So have we."

"But not with the chemical engines."

"Oh, well, I guess we can make out pretty well. Thank goodness, there's the grove. I'm almost melted."

The boys found a goodly crowd already assembled. The Jamesville fire department had arrived, and they greeted the Lakeville boys with cheers. Soon after this the Weedsport and Northville Centre contingents arrived.

Mr. Bergman had named a committee to see after the sports and games, and the members of this soon had things going. There were running races, walking matches, jumping contests, wheelbarrow and bag races, and tied-leg races, wherein two men, with their inner legs strapped together, did almost everything but run.

But what everyone was anxiously looking forward to were the fire drills. Though the boys of Lakeville took part in the other games, winning some of the contests, they waited with impatience for the main items on the program.

Very realistic contests had been arranged. In a big field, adjoining the grove, Mr. Bergman had caused to be erected six small sheds, constructed of old lumber, and filled with empty packing boxes. To make the fire burn more fiercely kerosene oil had been poured over the boxes.

The idea was to let the two companies of Lakeville have a chance first to see what they could do in the way of putting out a fire. They were to start from the same place, race toward the burning shacks, and the company which first put out the blaze was to be declared the winner. Then a four-cornered contest, among the Jamesville, Weedsport and Northville Centre firemen, and the winner of the Lakeville event, would strive for the honor of carrying home the silver trumpet.

When all was in readiness, with the two divisions of the Lakeville boys lined up at their respective machines, Mr. Bergman set fire to two of the shacks. In an instant they were enveloped in flames. Waiting until the fire was at its height, Mr. Bergman gave the word to start.

"Now, boys!" cried Bert to his men. "Show 'em how we do it!"

"Run! Run!" yelled Vincent, to his lads, "We want the chance to compete in the finals!"

With a rumble of the big wheels over the rough ground, the two chemical engines were hauled toward the blazes.

CHAPTER XIX

WINNING THE TRUMPET

Bert gave his lads the order to halt, when the engine was about fifty feet away from the burning shacks.

"Run out the hose!" he called to Tom Donnell. "The rest of you stand ready with the hooks, and, as soon as Tom has got her pretty near out, pull the boards apart so he can get out the last spark."

Quickly was the hose unreeled. Bert stood near the engine, ready to swing the lever and turn the valve wheel that would send the hot sulphuric acid into the soda water. Then, when there was a good head of gas accumulated in the cylinder, he would open another valve, and the fire-quenching fluid would spurt from the hose.

There was a hiss as the breaking of the glass holding the vitriol was followed by the instant generation of gas.

"Here she comes!" cried Bert, as he turned the valve.

A second later a white, foamy stream jetted from the nozzle, and sprayed into the midst of the blaze. The flames began to die down as if by magic.

But Vincent was not a second behind Bert in getting his machine into operation.

"Lively, boys!" he cried, and the hose was unreeled, the stream playing almost at the same instant as was Bert's.

The spectators set up a cheer. This was something few of them had seen. The chemical engines were proving what they could do. Whether the blaze at which Vincent's crew directed their stream was not as fierce as the other was not disclosed, but in spite of the fact that Bert's engine was the first in operation by a narrow margin, the blaze Vincent was fighting began to die down quicker.

"We'll win!" cried Vincent. "Our fire's out, and theirs is blazing good yet!"

A few seconds later, however, Tom Donnell had succeeded in taming the last of the leaping flames.

"Now, boys, tear her apart!" ordered Bert, and the lads with the long hooks began scattering the still glowing embers of the boards that had formed the shack. As soon as they did so, parts of the shed not touched by the chemical, began to blaze.

"Douse her, Tom!" cried the young chief, and Tom did so with good effect.

Meanwhile Vincent's crowd, thinking they had put their fire out, had turned away, while Vincent shut off the valve that controlled the outlet from the tank. No sooner had this been done than the fire in their shack blazed up again.

"Look!" cried John Boll, one of Vincent's crew.

"Turn on the stream!" shouted several of the lads. Vincent tried to do so, but before he could work it the shack was blazing again, almost as fiercely as before. He had been too confident that the fire was out.

By the time he got his stream to spurting again, Bert had the other fire completely out, so that only a little steam came from the pile of blackened embers.

"We win!" cried Cole Bishop.

"Yes, I guess you do," assented Mr. Bergman, who was the umpire. "I'll have to award you the decision. Now, Bert, fill your tank again, and get ready for the real contest, which will take place in about an hour."

"I'm glad you won, Bert," said Vincent, generously, coming over, and shaking hands with the young chief.

"Thanks. You see I thought the blaze was smouldering under the wood, and I was ready for it."

"I'll be, next time. I hope you win the trumpet."

"Well, so do I, for the sake of Lakeville. But these other departments have had more practice than we have."

All the members of the Lakeville fire corps turned in to help get Bert's engine ready for the main contest of the day. The tank was refilled with soda water, and a new bottle of sulphuric acid put in the holder, for a supply of the chemicals had been brought along for that purpose.

The other companies were also preparing for the contest. The Jamesville crowd had an engine just like these which Mr. Bergman had purchased for Lakeville. The machines from Northville Centre and Weedsport were different, but worked on the same principle.

"Are you all ready?" asked Mr. Bergman, when the four companies were lined up on the edge of the wood, ready for the race to the shacks. The various chiefs answered that they were. The word was given to fire the sheds, and soon four clouds of black smoke were ascending to the sky, while the flames began to roar.

"Don't start until I give the word," cautioned Mr. Bergman. "I want the fires to get a good headway."

Anxiously the members of the four companies stood lined up, ready for the signal. Grouped around them was a big throng.

"Be ready to jump, boys," cautioned Bert, in a low voice to his lads. "But be careful not to stumble."

"We're all ready," replied Cole, looking back at the line of boys who grasped the rope.

The flames were crackling more loudly. Greater clouds of smoke from the burning oil rolled into the air. The heat from the blazing shacks could be felt some distance away.

"Why doesn't he give the word?" asked Tom Donnell, impatiently.

Members of the other companies were inquiring the same thing. Mr. Bergman stood with his watch in his hand. He looked at the four fires. Then he called:

"Get ready!"

The boys tightened their grip on the rope. They leaned forward, prepared to spring at the command.

"Go!" shouted the umpire, and the four companies were off as one.

Over the open field they dragged the engines, the big wheels rumbling like subdued thunder. The crowd began to cheer, men and boys calling to their favorite companies to beat in the race.

Nearer and nearer to the blazing shacks came the fire-fighters. The company from Northville Centre was slightly in the lead, for their engine was lighter, and there were a score of men on the rope. Next came the Lakeville lads, while those from Weedsport were in the rear.

Suddenly there sounded a crash, and Bert, turning his head, saw the foremost of the Weedsport men stumble. An instant later the engine, striking a rut, overturned, dragging the whole company down.

"That—puts—them—out—of—the—-race!" panted Cole, who, in spite of his fleshiness, was keeping well up with his companions. But he was beginning to get out of breath. "We've—got—a—better—chance—now," he said.

"Don't talk," advised Bert. "Save your breath for running, Cole."

Which advice the young engineer followed.

It was now an even race between the Lakeville, Jamesville and Northville Centre departments. The members of the Weedsport crew were trying to right their engine.

"They've—got—her—up! They're—coming!" spoke Cole, as he looked back to see how their unfortunate adversaries fared. The three contestants were now about as close as they dared go to the blazes.

"Never mind them! We've got our own work cut out for us!" cried Bert. "Unreel, boys! I'll give you the stream as soon as you're ready!"

"Give it to us now!" cried Cole, quickly. "Turn the valve, Bert. The hose and nozzle will stand the pressure, and hold it back until we need it. Maybe we can beat 'em that way, for it will be there waiting for us."

Bert was a little doubtful, but he knew Cole was an authority on hose and nozzles. So, before the line was unreeled he had burst the sulphuric acid bottle, and the hissing within the tank told him the gas was beginning to generate.

"Come on, boys!" cried Cole, who, with Tom Donnell and several others, was pulling the long snake-like line of rubber toward the blaze which had been assigned to them to extinguish.

Cole's forethought proved successful. By the time the Lakeville boys were at the fire, the fluid had filled the hose, and was ready to spurt out of the nozzle. The others had waited until the hose was fully unreeled before putting the apparatus in operation.

"First stream!" yelled Cole with delight, as he saw the whitish fluid spurting toward the blaze.

They beat the other two companies by at least half a minute, and seconds count in these fire department contests.

But the fight was only begun. So fiercely were the shacks blazing that it seemed as if a big stream of water was needed to extinguish them. The small chemical ones did not appear adequate. But it was science triumphing over matter.

In less than a minute there was noticed a lessening in the power of all three blazes. The fourth one, assigned to the unfortunate Weedsport department, was going fiercely. But, with a shout, the members of that department, having righted their engine, which was only slightly damaged, rushed it up, and were soon playing a stream on the miniature conflagration.

"Well done!" shouted Bert, in praise of a gallant foe, and the chief of the Weedsport department acknowledged the compliment with a salute.

But the real contest was now among the Lakeville, Jamesville and Northville Centre crews. The two latter had taken a lesson from Bert's first contest, and had men ready with hooks to tear the piles apart as soon as chance offered.

This opportunity soon came, as the flames began to die down under the influence of the powerful gas.

"Tear it up, boys!" cried Bert, and, as his lads rushed forward, the men from the other departments did likewise. Once more the flames leaped up, as fresh material was thus made available, but the chemical streams made short work of them.

Misfortune seemed to follow the Weedsport department, for, when they had somewhat subdued their fire, something went wrong with their engine. No more fluid issued from the hose, and, with an explosion like that of a gun, the safety valve of the cylinder blew out, and the stream began spurting from the back.

"There's no fire there!" shouted the crowd, laughing at the bad luck of the Weedsport crew.

"Too bad, old man!" called Bert in sympathy.

"If he had my force-pump here, he could put out that fire yet," said Cole. "I wish our boys would run out the old hand-engine."

And that is exactly what the smaller lads did, at the suggestion of Mr. Bergman. He saw that the Weedsport department could do no more, and, as the water tank of the hand-engine had been filled, he thought of giving the smaller lads a chance to demonstrate what they could do. They rushed out, and soon had the blaze well in hand.

Meanwhile, the now triple-cornered contest was almost over. The three blazes were dying down. The lead which Bert and his lads had secured at the start, stood them in good stead. In a few minutes more, and just as the chemical in the tank began to give out, for Bert had, in the excess of his zeal, turned on full power, the blaze was extinguished. But, in the other two shacks, there were still signs of flames.

"Take up!" cried the chief, in his most professional voice.

The boys began to reel back the hose.

"Lakeville wins!" called the umpire of the contest.

"Hurrah! Three cheers for Lakeville!" yelled the crowd, and Bert and his lads blushed with pleasure, for they had won the silver trumpet.

CHAPTER XX

A FALSE ALARM

What a demonstration awaited the victors when they trundled their engine back to the grove! It seemed that every man from Lakeville wanted to shake hands with the boys.

"You've done the town more good than if you gave it a marble monument!" exclaimed Mayor Appelby, enthusiastically, as he greeted Herbert. "You've woke our sleepy village up, and I look for better times now. I'm going to run for mayor again. It's an honor."

"We'll see who'll be mayor," murmured Moses Sagger, who had come to the picnic after all. "If them boys think they can run things they'll find themselves very much mistaken."

The other engine companies, now that the fires were out, returned to the grove. They gathered around Bert and his lads, while Mr. Bergman, with a neat little speech, presented the young chief with a handsome silver trumpet.

"And while I wish you all success," he said in conclusion, "I also hope that through this trumpet you may give the order 'Take up' as quickly at every fire which occurs in Lakeville, as you did it to-day in this contest. You boys certainly worked fast, and I believe the 'devouring element,' as the poets call it, will take a back seat, now that we have such an efficient department to handle our two chemical engines."

"Hurrah for Lakeville!" yelled half a hundred voices.

"Three cheers for Mr. Bergman!" shouted others.

"Three cheers for the boys with the hand engine!" proposed Bert, for he wanted to encourage the little chaps.

"They couldn't have put that fire out if it hadn't been for my force-pump!" murmured Cole, amid the cheers that followed.

"Say, if you mention force-pump again to-day," threatened Tom Donnell, "we'll stand you up in front of it, and douse you good."

"Well, it's a fine pump," retorted Cole, taking care to get beyond Tom's reach.

There was more cheering and applause, the unfortunate Weedsport crew being given an extra cheer to make up for the bad luck it had encountered.

There were more games, a great dinner, some speech-making by the men, additional athletic contests among the firemen, and the picnic was brought to a close.

"Line up, Lakeville!" cried Herbert, through his trumpet. The boys manned the ropes of the three engines, including the old hand affair. They made a brilliant picture in their red shirts, blue trousers and shining helmets, and Bert proudly carried the glistening trophy where it would show to the best advantage.

With final cheers for each other the four fire departments separated, to march to their respective villages. It had been a great day, and, as Mr. Bergman had said, Lakeville had taken several steps forward in the way of progress.

"Well, we didn't do so bad," remarked Vincent to Bert, as they were on their way along the home road.

"No," replied the young chief, "but there's one thing we've got to look out for."

"What's that?"

"We must not use so much of the solution out of the tank. A small stream will do as much work, and it will last longer."

"That's so. We can't fill the tanks up very well while a fire is in progress."

"That's it. This afternoon, if the blaze had lasted a few minutes longer, there wouldn't have been any chemicals to squirt on it. It was my fault. I opened the valve too wide. We must remember that when we have a real fire."

As the young firemen entered the village, many, who had been to the picnic, but had come home early, crowded out to see them. The bells on the three engines clanged out in peals of victory, and when Bert started up a song, his comrades joined in with him.

As the two companies separated, one to go to the town hall, and the other to Cole's barn, a man stepped from the crowd, and approached Bert.

"Well, I see you won," he remarked pleasantly, and the young chief, looking up, saw the tramp he had rescued from the water.

"Yes. Were you there?"

"I saw the final contest. Couldn't get away to spend the whole day, though I would have liked to. I had to work."

"Where are you working? In town here?" asked Bert, for he was quite interested in the young man.

"Yes, I'm employed at the Stockton mansion."

"At the Stockton mansion?" repeated Bert, greatly surprised. What he had heard regarding that mysterious house came freshly to his mind. "Why, I didn't know there was any business being done there, Mr.—er—Mr. ah—"

He paused, for it just occurred to him that he did not know the tramp's name.

The tramp—no, we shall call him that no more, for he was no longer of that class—the man, then, smiled.

"Decker is my name," he said. "Mortimer Decker, though most of my friends—what few I have left—call me Mort. As I consider you a friend of mine, you may do so, Herbert. You see I know your name, for you're sort of a public character."

"I don't know about that, but I'm glad you've gotten a place, Mort."

"Yes, after my little experience in the brook I decided to get some work to do here if possible. I heard that the man who lived in that big mansion was rich, and I thought he might want a private secretary, or a stenographer and typewriter. I learned who lived there, but when I inquired at the place an old woman said Mr. Stockton had gone away."

"I believe he has, but there seems to be something queer about it," said Bert. "No one saw him go, and, though he never used to be seen much around the village, still we did have occasional glimpses of him. Now no one has seen him for some time."

"So it appears. But the old woman—Blarcum, she said her name was—called a young man to talk to me. He was Alfred Muchmore, Mr. Stockton's nephew, and, after I had told him what I could do, he engaged me."

"I didn't think he had any work you could do," said Bert, recalling the rumor he had heard, that Muchmore was a professional gambler.

"Well, he has quite a lot of business papers to copy, and I am doing that for him. He pays me well. Still, I can't say that I altogether like the place."

"Why not?"

Mort Decker came closer to Herbert, though no one was then near them, the boys of the department being too interested in cleaning the engine, refilling it, and putting it in the barn, to pay attention to anything else.

"There's something queer about that house," said Mort in a whisper.

"Queer? How do you mean?"

"Well, Muchmore seems afraid that I will go into some rooms where I have no business. Once I was going down a long corridor, when he called me back, and said those were his private apartments, and no one was allowed there. Then, again, I was just going into a room that the old housekeeper said contained fine paintings, for I am very fond of pictures, but Mr. Muchmore thrust me back, and seemed quite excited. Then, too, the housekeeper seems very much afraid of the young nephew. I believe there is some secret connected with that house."

"So do I," declared Bert, and he told Mort of his experience when the fire had occurred.

"I'll keep my eyes open, and see if I can learn anything," promised the stenographer. "If I hear anything I'll let you know. I can't invite you to call and see me, for I'm afraid Muchmore wouldn't like it. But the first chance I get I'll come down and see you."

"I wish you would," replied Bert. "You'll generally find me at one of the engine houses, at least until school opens. Then I've got to begin my studies again."

"Well, good-bye," said Mort, as he left, while Bert went to the barn, to see that the chemical tank was properly filled, in readiness for an alarm.

As yet, beyond the one blaze in a small shed in the village, the engines had not been tested at a real fire, nor had the new alarm system been called on to show how much of an aid it was in enabling the department to respond quickly. Several boxes had been installed in different parts of the town, all running to the two fire-houses, as the basement of the town hall and Cole's barn were designated. By means of a simple switchboard arrangement, and a code of signals, given on a gong, it could be told at once which box was pulled. In addition the new bell on the tall steel tower would ring an alarm to awaken those members of the department who were asleep at home.

There was a short meeting of the fire department one night, in Cole's barn, where various matters were talked over, and the boys had not dispersed more than an hour, when there sounded an alarm from the tower. At the same time there rang out on the apparatus in Cole's barn, the number of a box located near the Stockton mansion.

"There's another fire at the house of mystery," cried Cole, for the boys had given the mansion that designation. "Come on, fellows. Let's see if we can't do better this time than we did with our hand engine."

While he was speaking he was drawing on his rubber boots, for, like his companions, he had gotten ready for bed. Before the alarm had ceased ringing (for it sounded the box number automatically four times, once it was started) the engine was being pulled out of quarters.

There were only eight boys on duty in the barn, and the task of pulling the heavy engine up the hill to the Stockton mansion was not easy. But, before they were half way there, they were met by several of their comrades, who grabbed the rope.

"Come on! Come on!" yelled Bert, who was among the first to arrive from home. "Don't let the fire get too much of a start!"

They toiled on, and, as they rounded a and came in sight of the big house, there was not a sign of fire.

"That's queer," remarked the young chief. "I wonder if there's something wrong with the signal apparatus."

"What's the matter, boys? Out for a practice drill?" asked a voice, and Herbert and his chums saw, in the glare from the lamps on the engine, Mr. Alfred Muchmore coming out of the driveway that led to the big house.

"We came in response to a fire alarm," said Bert, "but I don't see any blaze."

"Blaze? There isn't any. I don't understand it. I don't want you boys around here. You'd better leave."

That was rather queer, coming from a man to whom they expected to be of service. Bert and his chums were puzzled.

"False alarm! False alarm!" suddenly yelled a voice from the bushes that lined the roadway. "I sent it in, you old miser, to get even with you! Maybe you'll say 'Thanks' next time, Mr. Muchmore, when we put out a real fire in your place," and a lad, whom Bert recognized as rather an undesirable character about the village, dashed from the shrubbery, and ran off down the road, laughing at the trick he had played.

Frank V. Webster

CHAPTER XXI

THE MYSTERIOUS MESSAGE

The unexpected announcement by the daring lad, of what he had done, was a surprise to both Mr. Muchmore and the members of the fire department.

"So, this is a trick by one of you young rascals, is it?" asked the rich man's nephew. "I shall take action against you for this. The road you are on is private property, and I shall have you arrested if you do not, at once, cease from trespassing on it. Get out of here with your noisy apparatus!"

"Mr. Muchmore," said Bert firmly, "you are mistaken when you think that our fire department had anything to do with this false alarm. We regret it as much as you do. We came here because we believed there was a fire. The box located near here was pulled."

"I shall take steps to see that it is not rung again. I shall have it removed," said the man. "Now I order you to clear out!"

"We will," replied the young chief, "but I want to say that no member of our department had anything to do with annoying you."

"You heard what that young rascal said. That he did it to pay me for not thanking you boys for what you did at the other fire. That was an oversight. I was too excited, I suppose, but that is hardly an excuse for disturbing me in this way."

"Mr. Muchmore," exclaimed Bert, "the boy who sent in the false alarm is not a member of our department. He never was, though he might have helped at the other fire."

"Well, it seems strange that I can't live here in peace and quietness, without being annoyed by a lot of boys," retorted Muchmore. "Perhaps you knew nothing of the false alarm—"

"I assure you we did not. We don't care enough about this long run uphill to undertake it on a false alarm," declared Bert.

"That's right," added Cole.

"Very well, then you had better go down. As for that boy who pulled the box, I shall take steps to have him arrested."

"If you will, you would be doing us a service," replied Bert. "We don't want false alarms to be sent in, and if that boy— Chester Randel is his name—finds out he is liable to arrest, it may serve as a warning to others."

"I'll see about it," and, without thanking the boys for their promptness in coming to put out a possible fire, Muchmore turned back, and went up the private driveway to the big house, that stood dark and silent on the hill.

"This is one on us," remarked Cole, as he helped to drag the engine around. "I'd like to wallop Chester."

"So would I," declared Bert. "Mr. Muchmore will attend to him, though, I guess."

"Muchmore needs someone to attend to him, too," remarked Tom Donnell. "He's as cross as a couple of sour apple trees. I guess if the house had been on fire he'd have been only too glad to see us."

Still the boys did not so much mind their useless run, as they were so enthusiastic over their engine and the new department that it had not yet become an old story to them.

"We were in need of a little practice, anyhow," remarked Bert, as they backed the engine into the barn. The second apparatus had not responded, though the boys were in readiness to run it out in case a call came for them.

When he got back home that night Herbert was racking his brains over the mystery that seemed to surround the Stockton mansion. That there was something queer going on within its walls he was positive. What he had seen, Muchmore's queer actions, his fear of something being discovered, and what Mort Decker had told him, convinced Bert that very unusual proceedings must be taking place in the silent house on the hill.

"Mr. Stockton ought to be informed," he said. "I wonder if I couldn't send a letter to him? I've a good notion to make some inquiries at the post-office."

He did, the next day. As he entered the post-office he saw that Mr. Daven was busy reading some postal cards.

"Ah, how d'ye do, Bert?" he greeted, for he had a kindly feeling for the lad, who, in a measure, was responsible for the awakening of the town. "How's the fire business?"

"Pretty good. We had a run for nothing last night."

"I heard about that. Up to the Stockton mansion. Yes, I may have to take official action on it."

"How's that?"

"Why, Mr. Muchmore was in here a while ago. He came to see me in my official capacity as justice of the peace, and not postmaster. He wanted a warrant for the arrest of Chester

Randel, and I made out one. The next thing is to arrest that good-for-nothing lad, but he's like a flea, I never can catch him when I want him. I've got another warrant for him too."

"What's that for?"

"Oh, he robbed Deacon Stanton's apple orchard. Not that taking apples is such a crime, but the deacon insisted on a warrant, and I had to make one out."

"Are you going to arrest Chester?"

"If I can catch him, but I'm so busy with mail lately that I ain't got much time to arrest anybody. 'Pears everybody is sending out souvenir postals, with pictures of the new engines on 'em, and it takes a lot of time to read and sort 'em."

An enterprising stationer in town had ordered a supply of postals made, with pictures of the new fire apparatus, and he sold quite a number. Bert thought the postmaster's talk gave him a good opening to ask certain questions.

"I wonder if Mr. Stockton knows about our new department?" he said. "I'd like to send him one of those postals, though I don't really know him very well. Still, I think he would be interested. Do you know his address?"

"No, Bert, I don't."

"I heard he had gone to Europe."

"Maybe he has, but I can't say."

"Do you get any letters for him?"

"Yes, quite a few."

"Then don't you forward them?"

"No, for I don't know where to send them. Besides, that nephew of his calls for the mail, and takes the letters addressed to Mr. Stockton, as well as his own. I don't believe Mr. Stockton is in Europe."

"Then where is he?"

"That's more than I know, Bert. It's something I don't have time to bother about, with the increase in the mail, and my eyesight getting poorer and poorer each day. I can't read as many postals as I used to."

"Then if I wrote a letter to Mr. Stockton, you don't think he'd get it?"

"I don't know. I do know that Muchmore would get it first. Maybe he forwards his uncle's mail."

"I don't believe I'll write any letter then," thought Bert. "I have nothing only suspicions, at best. I think something wrong is going on at that house, but I can't prove it. I think Mr. Stockton ought to know about it, but I don't see any way of informing him. I wish I could have a talk with Mort Decker. Maybe he has found out something."

Once he got thinking in this strain Bert found it hard to get his mind off the matter. As he had nothing in particular to do, he decided to take a stroll past the mysterious mansion. He knew of a road, through the woods, that would bring him to the rear of the house, without any one seeing him.

He started off, passing through the back streets of the village, as he did not want to meet any of his chums just then. In a little while he was in the forest, and, proceeding along leisurely, so that if any persons did observe him they would not think he had any particular object, he reached the rear of the queer house. It seemed to be deserted. The shutters on the back were tightly closed, and there was no sign of life.

"A queer old place," mused the boy. "I wonder what—"

His musing was cut short by a sudden opening of the shutters on the topmost window. They were thrown violently back, as though whatever fastened them had been broken. At the same moment a hand was thrust out. It was a white hand, and it seemed to throw something from the window. Bert watched, and saw that the object was a bottle. The glass struck a stone and was broken. Then, from the bottle came a piece of white paper. The shutters were closed again. Wonderingly, Bert walked over and picked up the paper. On it was this mysterious message:

"help i am a priso"

CHAPTER XXII

THE STENOGRAPHER'S SUSPICIONS

Herbert stood gazing at the slip of paper in his hand. He did not know what to make of it. Then he looked up at the window whence it had been thrown. There was no sign of life there. Whoever had tossed out the mysterious message had disappeared again behind the dark shutters.

"Well, this gets me," murmured the boy. "I wonder what it means? Is it a joke; or something serious?"

Then another idea came to him.

"It's written on a typewriter!" he exclaimed. "I wonder if it could have been done by Mort Decker? Perhaps he is in trouble there with Muchmore. Maybe the man has him locked up. Had I better tell the authorities?"

Then, as he looked at the message again, he had a different thought.

"No, Mort couldn't have written it," he said to himself. "He knows how to work a typewriter, and he'd use capitals in the places where they belong. And, besides, this message isn't finished. Whoever wrote it had to stop before he was through. I wonder what the rest of that word is. 'Priso—' Maybe it's meant for 'poisoned' and it's spelled wrong. I wish—"

But the boy's thoughts were suddenly interrupted by a noise at a window over his head. Thinking the person who had thrown out the mysterious message was again about to open the shutters, Bert watched anxiously, but, instead, a window on the second floor opened and Mort Decker leaned out.

"Hello!" began Bert.

"Hush!" exclaimed Mort, placing his fingers over his lips as an additional signal of caution. "Get away from here, Bert; Mr. Muchmore is coming!"

"But," went on the boy, "I have—"

"Don't say a word. Hurry away. I'll try to see you to-night, at the barn. Go, before—"

He did not finish the sentence, but hurriedly shut the shutters, and closed the window. Bert took the hint, and glided into the woods, where he could not be observed. He gave one look back at the mysterious house, and once more he saw that the window, from which Mort had looked, was open. But the stenographer did not peer forth. Instead, the face of Muchmore appeared. The man looked around carefully, as if to see if anyone had been communicating with inmates of the house. Then, apparently satisfied, as he saw nothing suspicious, he pulled the shutters tightly together, and closed the window.

"Well, things are happening in a bunch," thought Bert, as he made his way toward the village. "First I get a queer message I can't make head or tail of, and then Mort warns me away from the house. I wonder what he wants to tell me to-night? It must have something to do with the Stockton place."

Bert almost wished that a fire alarm might come in, so that the time would pass more quickly. But the day dragged along, and there was no occasion for taking out either of the engines.

After supper, as was his custom, the young chief visited the two fire-houses, to see that both apparatuses were in readiness for a run in the night. The tanks were kept filled, and the lanterns were lighted as soon as it grew dark.

Bert first went to the town hall, where, in the basement, he found Vincent and several members of "Corps No. 2," as it was known.

"Well, boys, all ready for a blaze?" asked Bert. "How's the machine, Vincent?"

"All right, I guess. We thought we were going to have a run, a while ago."

"How's that?"

"Pile of shavings near Sagger's new butcher shop caught fire, and made a lot of smoke. He came running in here, and wanted us to take the engine out, but I saw it didn't amount to anything, and I didn't want to waste a lot of chemicals on a blaze like that."

"What did you do?"

"We put it out with a few pails of water. He could have done the same, only he was too excited."

"And he is the man who said the bucket brigade was good enough," observed John Boll.

"I guess he's changed his mind," remarked Bert. "I'm going over to Cole's barn," he added. "It's my night on duty."

Bert found Cole and several of his chums engaged in games of checkers and dominoes in the barn, which had been fitted up as much as possible like a fire-house. Bert greeted his chums, and then sat down, to await, with what patience he could, the promised arrival of Mort.

"I hope he comes," thought the boy. "I'd like to get at the bottom of this."

It was nearly nine o'clock when Mort looked in at the open door of the barn and nodded to Bert.

"I'll be back in a little while, boys," said the young chief, as he followed the stenographer outside. There was an oil lamp in the driveway leading to the street, and Bert, pausing under it, pulled out the queer slip of paper, and showed it to Mort.

"I thought maybe you might know something about this," he said.

"Where did you get it?"

"I picked it up right near where you saw me, under the window. Some one threw it out."

"So, that's why you were there, eh? I couldn't imagine. I thought you were trying to find out something about that house of mystery."

"So I was. Why did you warn me away?"

"Because, as I told you, Muchmore was right there. I happened to see you when I was at work, in the place he has fitted up as an office, and I didn't want you to get into trouble. You were on his private land, and he would just as soon as not have you arrested."

"I'm not afraid of that. But what do you make of this message?"

Mort, who had not closely examined the paper before, started as he caught sight of it.

"Why, that was written on my typewriter!" he exclaimed. "I mean on the one Muchmore bought for me to use. I can tell, because the letter 'e' prints a little bit out of alignment."

"Who wrote it?" asked Bert. "What do you make of it?"

"I don't know who wrote it. Some one must have gone to my typewriter when I was away, or maybe it was done at night."

"Could it have been the old housekeeper?" asked Bert. "Maybe she is in trouble, and this looks like an appeal for aid."

"No. Mrs. Blarcum is afraid to touch the machine. Besides, she doesn't even know how to put the paper in."

"Muchmore wouldn't have tossed out a message like that, I suppose?"

"No. Besides, he knows how to work the machine, and he'd use the proper lettering. Anyhow, he'd have no occasion to do such a thing."

"Then what can it be?" inquired Bert, much puzzled.

"Certainly someone is in trouble," agreed Mort. "The word 'help' shows that. Properly written the message would look like this, and on the back of the paper he wrote:

"Help! I am a priso"

"What's that last word?" asked Bert. "I thought it might have been meant for 'poison.' What do you think?"

Mort was silent a moment. Then he exclaimed:

"I have it! It's 'prisoner'! That's what it is!"

"Prisoner?"

"Yes."

"But who could be imprisoned there?"

"I don't know. Maybe it's a lunatic, or some poor fellow whom Muchmore has fleeced out of all his money by gambling."

"Then he is a gambler?"

"Yes; but how did you know?"

"Well, it is rumored so in the village."

"Yes. He is a gambler, and something more. I believe he is a worse criminal. He has had several gambling parties at his house. Men come after dark, in automobiles, along the private road. Sometimes they arrive in the motor boat from the other side of the lake. They don't pass through the village at all. Oh, I see and hear things that Muchmore never suspects I know about."

"But what makes you think he is a criminal?"

"Because he has had me doing some queer work lately."

"What kind?"

"Making copies of old deeds and mortgages. Now, no man has deeds and mortgages copied unless he is going to dispose of property, and all this property is in the name of Harris Stockton, his uncle. I believe Muchmore is up to some crooked game."

"But where is Mr. Stockton?"

"That's what I can't find out. Muchmore says he is in Europe, and I often write for him letters addressed to his uncle, which are directed to different cities in France and Germany. But Muchmore always mails them himself. I don't know where Mr. Stockton is. If I did I'd send him word of what is going on in his house, and what I suspect his nephew is up to."

"But what about this queer message?" asked Bert.

"I'm sure I don't know what to say. There is some mystery about it. I will try and get on the track of it, but to do that I must get up on the top floor, and that is a place Muchmore carefully guards. Perhaps you can help me."

"I'm afraid not, but I'll try."

"Do," urged the stenographer. "I'll see you again, and—"

At that instant the fire alarm began ringing, and Bert rushed back to the barn.

CHAPTER XXIII

A BRAVE RESCUE

"Run her out, boys!" cried Bert. "It's the box at Needham's factory. If the factory gets going it'll be the worst fire we ever had in this town!"

Needham's factory was one where boxes for various purposes were made, and it was filled with inflammable material. The young firemen needed no urging. They sprang to their places. The bell on the engine sent out its warning note, as they wheeled the machine from the barn. The reel clicked as the long rope was unwound.

"Come on!" cried Bert, as he took his place at the head of the line.

"That's the way to run her out!" exclaimed the stenographer admiringly, as the boys swept past him.

"I'll see you again!" Bert called to him, for the thoughts of the young chief were now entirely upon the fire to which he was going.

"All right," answered Mort Decker. "I'll call around to-morrow."

Out into the street rushed the lads, dragging the engine after them. The tower bell, with quick, sharp strokes, was sounding the alarm. The noise of rushing feet could be heard, as men and boys hurried toward the blaze.

"We'll need the other engine, if the factory is on fire," commented Cole, who was beginning to lose his breath as the swift pace was kept up.

"Yes," answered Bert. "Vincent knows he's to answer all alarms near dangerous places without waiting for a special call. He'll be there before we are."

This was because the second engine was on the side of town nearest the factory.

"Maybe it isn't the box place," suggested Tom Donnell.

"I—hope—not," spoke Cole, laboredly.

"The factory is the nearest building to the alarm box," said Bert, "but of course the using of that box doesn't mean that the factory is on fire."

"Something is blazing, anyhow," added Tom. "I can see the reflection."

On the sky shone a lurid light, and there was the smell of burning wood in the air, as the wind blew toward the lads. On they rushed, the warning bell on the engine clanging loudly, and mingling with the rumble of the big wheels. It was a fine sight, and one would have enjoyed seeing the sturdy lads hurrying along, with the brightly polished engine sparkling in the light of the four lamps on it, had it not been for the thought of the fire which was destroying property, and, possibly, endangering life.

"It is the box factory!" suddenly cried Tom, as they turned a corner, and saw the blaze in plain sight.

"That's right!" added Bert. "Vincent and his boys are on hand.

Put a little more steam on, fellows!"

Several of their comrades had joined them on the way, some not stopping to don their uniforms, while a few were only half dressed. It was easier work hauling the engine now.

"It's got a good start," remarked Bert. "I'm afraid we can't save much. We'll need the old hand-engine, too."

"Here it comes," cried Tom, as another rumble was heard, and the clumsy tank machine, manned by a score of smaller lads, came down a side street.

The factory was blazing furiously. It was not a big building, but it was filled with dry wood, which made excellent fuel for the flames. A big crowd had gathered in front, and a number of men were aiding Vincent's lads in saving as much of the finished stock as they could carry out from a side door, which the flames had not yet reached.

"Jump in and save as much as you can!" ordered Bert. "Unreel, Cole! Tom? take the nozzle as close as possible! I'll give you the full pressure at once. You'll need all you can get for this fire!"

Vincent's engine already had a chemical stream on the blaze, and it was doing effective work wherever the fluid was directed. But quite an area was now blazing.

There was a hiss as the gas began to form in the copper cylinder when Bert turned the valve, and an instant later a second whitish stream was being directed at the licking tongues of fire.

"If—we—only—had—my—force—pump!" panted Cole, who had not yet recovered his breath.

"Looks as if we were going to have it!" exclaimed Bert, as the old hand-engine was wheeled up, and the boys, with some men to aid them, formed a bucket line, and prepared to work

Frank V. Webster

the handles, while the three lengths of hose, including the one from Cole's force-pump, were run out.

"Shall we start in, Bert?" cried Fred Newton, who constituted himself captain of the hand-engine company.

"Let her go!" yelled the chief through his trumpet, for it needed a strong voice to be heard above the din.

The young firemen were doing fine work. As it needed but two lads on the two lines of chemical hose, the others could turn their attention to saving property. They managed to get out a large quantity of the finished boxes, some of which were for holding jewelry, and were very expensive. Two members of the firm had arrived by this time, and helped in saving some valuable papers from the office, which was almost destroyed.

The chemical streams were beginning to have an effect on the fire, which seemed to be dying down. The three streams of water from the hand-engine were also of good service.

Suddenly there was a sound of a loud explosion.

"That's in the varnish department!" exclaimed Mr. Needham. "Look out, everybody! There are barrels of alcohol and turpentine in there! They'll blow the whole place up! Better get back, boys," he added. "You can't save the factory!"

"We're not going to give up!" answered Bert. "There is plenty of the solution left in the tanks, and we can charge them again in five minutes. We've got plenty of acid and soda."

At that moment there was another explosion, louder than the first.

"That's a barrel of turpentine!" cried Mr. Needham. "Get back, boys!"

But the young firemen pluckily stuck to their task. It was so hot that they had to cease trying to save any more of the boxes, and even the lads with the hose had to move back from the fierce flames. But they did not give up.

Suddenly there was a cry of horror, and a score of hands pointed upward. There, on the roof of an extension of the factory, that was just beginning to blaze, stood a man.

"It's the watchman!" cried Mr. Needham. "He has his apartments there. He must have gone back to get something and the flames have trapped him!"

"What has he got in his arms?" asked Bert.

"In his arms? I don't know. Must be some of his things."

"It's a little girl! A little girl!" shouted the young chief.

"His niece! I remember now," said Mr. Needham. "She lived there with him. Oh, why did he go back? He was safe, for I was talking to him a few minutes ago, in front of the factory."

"Perhaps he went back to get the little girl," suggested Bert. "But he's in danger now."

The young chief ran forward, telling Cole to look after the engine. As he did so sheets of flame burst from the windows of the extension, on which the aged watchman stood.

"Get a ladder!" shouted Bert. "It's the only way he can get down! Fetch a ladder, boys!"

One was found, and quickly raised against the extension in a place where the flames had not yet broken out. Bert was up it in a second, while some of his comrades held the end on the ground, to steady it.

"Come on! I'll help you down!" cried Bert to the old man.

"I—I can't!" was the quavering answer, "I've got rheumatism so I can hardly move, and I'm stiff from fright!"

"You must!" insisted Bert. "This place will be all ablaze in another minute! Here, give me the little girl! I'll carry her down, and help you!"

"You—you can't do it!"

"Yes, I can. Give her to me! Come on!"

Bert took off his coat. Then he wrapped the little girl, who was motionless from fright, in the garment. Next he tied the sleeves together, making a bundle with the little girl inside, but leaving an opening through which she could breathe. Then, holding the precious burden in one arm, with the other he assisted the old man toward the edge of the roof.

"Go down the ladder!" cried the young chief.

"I can't!" complained the aged watchman.

"You must. The roof is giving way! Quick!"

The man gave one frightened look back, and then, trembling with fear, he started to descend the ladder.

"Don't—don't drop the child!" he called to Bert.

"I'll not! Hurry! It's getting too hot here!"

The flames were now coming through the roof of the extension. When the man was part way down the ladder, Bert, holding the little girl close to him, started to follow.

"Give him a hand!" he cried to some of the young firemen on the ground, and two of them came up the rounds to aid the watchman.

The old man reached the ground in safety, and Bert, with the child, was half way down the ladder when, from a window, past which he would have to climb, there burst out a terrible sheet of flame.

Frank V. Webster

CHAPTER XXIV

AN ENCOUNTER WITH MUCHMORE

For an instant the crowd was horror-struck. It seemed that the brave young chief, and the little girl, must perish. For it was next to impossible to pass through that sheet of flame unharmed. The mass of superheated air, generated by the varnishes and other material in the extension, was forcing the flame out from the window in the shape of a great fan. The ladder was beginning to blaze.

Bert paused and looked down to the ground. The distance was not too great for him to jump, had he been alone, but, with the child, it might mean that both would be seriously injured.

"Throw her to me!" yelled Mr. Needham, and, at that, several men stretched out their arms, ready to catch the burden. But Bert shook his head. He did not want to run any risk of anyone not catching the little one, for he would have to toss her, with considerable force, away from the building, to have her escape the flames.

Yet there seemed to be no other way. Oh, how he wished the new department had a life net! He made up his mind he would soon get one, if he came out of this situation alive.

But Vincent had seen his chum's peril, and at once a daring plan came to him. The chemical stream from his engine, as well as that from the other, and the three water jets from the hand apparatus, were still playing on the flames.

"This way!" yelled Vincent. "Use what chemicals you have left, and all the water you can pump on the fire in the extension. That'll keep the flames from the window long enough for him to get past." The others caught the idea at once, and the boys rushed with their lines of hose around to where Bert still stood on the ladder, that was now ablaze in several places.

With a hiss like that of an angry snake, the flames seemed to shrink back at the touch of the elements to which they were opposed. The fan of fire, shooting from the windows, appeared to die down, almost at once.

"Come on! Come on!" cried the crowd to Bert, and, seeing his chance, he climbed farther down the ladder. Just as he reached the place opposite the window, the flames once more shot out. But he ducked down, and a well-directed stream, from the hose attached to Cole's force-pump, sent a saving spray over the brave lad and the little girl. The fire on the ladder was quenched, and, as that from the window was driven back, Bert made the rest of the descent in safety. Cole's pump had proved its worth.

A score of hands reached out to take the burden from Herbert, but he gently put them aside, and placed the little girl in her uncle's arms.

Then what a cheer there was for the brave young chief's act! But Bert had other things to do than listen to praises of himself.

"How are the engines, boys?" he asked.

"Pretty well run out," answered Vincent.

"Well, get ready to make some more solution. Shut down one engine, and fill the tank, and then do the same for the other. We'll fight this fire to a finish!"

This was done, and soon, with replenished tanks, the two pieces of apparatus were again in use. The old hand-engine, too, did its share, and so energetically did the young firemen attack the blaze, that at last the fire sullenly gave up.

"I think we've got it under control," said Bert, as he saw the flames beginning to die down. "If we don't have any more explosions, we'll be all right."

Fortunately there were no more, and, though the factory was badly damaged, the larger part of it was saved. But that was nothing compared to the satisfaction the members of the department felt over Bert's brave act.

In an hour more the last spark had been extinguished, and the chief gave orders for the engines to go back to quarters. It was the worst fire they had yet undertaken to fight, and the new engines had proved their efficiency in no uncertain manner. Little was talked of in town, the next day, but the fire and the sensational rescue.

As for Bert and his chums, they, too, had a fruitful subject for conversation. They had learned much from their experience at the box factory blaze, which was liable to stand them in good stead at future fires.

"I heard about you," remarked Mort Decker to Bert, when the next night he called at Cole's barn. "First thing you know you'll be getting offers from some big city department."

"Oh, I guess not. But how are things at the house of mystery? Have you discovered anything new?"

The two had walked out from the barn, to converse alone.

"I don't like the way things are going," replied the stenographer. "Muchmore gave me several other deeds to copy to-day, and in some he had me change the descriptions and names. I don't like it. I'm sure, now, that he is a crook."

"Can you do anything?"

"That's just what I was thinking about. I have an idea he has some person a prisoner on that top floor, whom he is holding there until that person does as he wants, in the matter of some property."

"If we could only get word to Mr. Stockton," said Bert, "he might call in the authorities."

"Yes, if we could, that would be the very thing. But I don't know how to do it. I wrote him a letter, and mailed it in the post-office, but a little later I saw it on Muchmore's table. He must get Mr. Stockton's mail, and forward it. And now I think Muchmore suspects me, because he probably opened that letter I wrote to his uncle. So we may as well take the bull by the horns, and do something."

"Yes; but what?"

Mort looked around to see that no one would overhear him.

"I'm going to make a try to get on that top floor," he said, "and I want you to help me."

"When are you going to do it?"

"To-night, in a little while. Muchmore is away, and there's nobody but the housekeeper there. We'll see who that mysterious prisoner is, who sends out typewritten messages asking for help. Will you come?"

"Sure. I don't have to stay here. It's my night off."

"Then come up to the Stockton mansion in about an hour. Go to the side door, knock three times, then a pause, then twice, and I'll know it's you, and let you in. We'll see if we can't solve the mystery."

About an hour after this conversation Bert knocked at the door of the big house as directed. The place seemed deserted, and there was not a ray of light to be seen.

"I wonder if he's here, or if Muchmore found out what he was up to, and drove him out," thought Bert, as he waited for an answer. But in a few minutes the stenographer admitted him.

"Don't make any noise," he cautioned. "Mrs. Blarcum is in her room, but she has good hearing in spite of her age, and I think she is somehow mixed up with the mystery. Now we'll go to the top floor," and he took up a big poker, which was on a chair in the side hall.

"What's that for?" asked Bert.

"We may have to smash down a door or two, or pry them open. This is the only thing I could find. Now come on."

They cautiously ascended the stairs. When they reached the top floor, they found a stout door barring their progress. Mort Decker tried to insert the point of the poker in the lock, to force it, but, finding he could not do this, he raised the heavy iron, to break the panels.

At the first blow there sounded from the other side of the portal a cry:

"Help! Help! Let me out!"

"Who are you? Why arc you in there?" asked Mort, pausing in his attack on the door.

Before he could distinguish the answer, if one was made, there sounded from behind the two rescuers, a woman's scream, and they turned to see Mrs. Blarcum rushing at them.

"Come away from there!" she cried. "Come away! Mr. Muchmore doesn't allow any one there!"

"I don't care what he allows!" retorted Mort. "We're going to get at the bottom of this mystery!"

Once more he rained a shower of blows on the door.

"Get away from there!" cried the old woman, rushing up, and grabbing the stenographer by the arm. "Help! Help!" she added. "Mr. Muchmore, he is breaking down the door to the secret corridor!"

Suddenly there sounded from below the rush of feet. Then came a startled cry.

"I'm coming!" some one shouted.

"Muchmore! It's Muchmore!" exclaimed Mort, pausing. "If he finds us here—"

"Let's stick it out!" urged Bert bravely. "We'll find out what this means!"

An instant later, Muchmore, his face distorted with anger, rushed upon them.

CHAPTER XXV

THE MYSTERY SOLVED—CONCLUSION

"Get away from that door!" yelled the enraged man. "What right have you to be prying into my affairs? I hired you to do copying work for me, not to roam about this house."

"Well, I'm done copying those illegal deeds for you!" retorted Mort. "And, what's more, we're going to find out whom you have a prisoner in there!"

"A prisoner? You are joking. There is no one in there."

"Yes, there is. He wrote an appeal for help on the typewriter and tossed the paper from the window. Hark, you can hear him calling for help!"

There was a moment's silence, but no cry came from behind the door, one panel of which was shattered.

"You see," sneered Muchmore. "I guess you'll wish you hadn't begun this work, my friend, before I'm through with you. You'll be in jail ere you are many hours older. As for you," went on the man, turning to Bert, "I warned you, once before, not to trespass on my property. I shall also make a complaint against you. Now, clear out, both of you!"

"Suppose I refuse to go?" asked Mort coolly.

"Then I'll throw you out. I paid you your wages to the end of the week. You can consider yourself dismissed. If you don't go—"

Muchmore paused, but there was such a fierce look on his face, as he strode toward Bert and the stenographer, that, though neither of them was a coward, they judged it best not to provoke the man too much.

"Oh, we'll go," replied the stenographer. "But I warn you that you haven't heard the last of this. This place will be searched, by the proper authorities, and that prisoner, whoever he is, will be released."

"There is no prisoner there," retorted Muchmore. "And I'd like to see the authorities here, or from anywhere else, search this house without my permission. A man's house is his castle, here as much as in England. Now you have my answer, and you can do your worst!"

"I'll inform Mr. Stockton," threatened Bert.

"Do, you young rascal, when you can find him," and, with a laugh, Muchmore motioned his two unwelcome visitors to leave.

"Well, we didn't find out much," remarked the stenographer, as he and Bert were descending the hill toward the village. "I'm afraid I made rather a mess of it. He came back unexpectedly."

"Maybe he never went away."

"Mrs. Blarcum said he was going to be gone all night."

"I believe she's in with him. But we certainly learned one thing. Some person is a prisoner in the house, and it's a man who wants to get out."

"And we'll help him," added Mort. "I'll inform the authorities in the morning."

"Where will you stay to-night?" asked Bert.

"I don't know. I guess I'll go to the hotel."

"It isn't a very good place. Better come to my house. There are only mother and I, and we have a spare room for you."

"You are very kind. I'll come."

Mrs. Dare welcomed the stenographer, and, after he and Bert had talked over the queer events of the evening, they went to bed, intending to start an official inquiry the first thing in the morning.

But fate took a hand in the matter, and the mystery was solved sooner than Bert or Mort expected it would be.

In the middle of the night there was an alarm of fire. It came from the box on the hill, near the Stockton mansion, and Bert, hearing the clanging of the bell on the tower, awoke with a start and began to dress.

"Where is the blaze?" asked Mort.

"Somewhere up near the house of mystery. I hope it isn't another false alarm."

"May I go with you?" asked the stenographer.

"Of course. Hurry."

Mort quickly dressed, and he and Bert, the latter making his usual promise to his mother that he would be careful, were soon hastening from the house, and toward the location of the box, where they would meet the engine.

"It's no false alarm!" exclaimed Mort, as they began to climb the hill leading to the big house.

"You're right. It's a fire, but it doesn't seem to be very big. The engine is there; I can hear the bell."

Bert and the stenographer had taken a short cut to the Stockton mansion, and, as they emerged from the woods, on that side of the house where Bert had picked up the mysterious message, they saw flames shooting from one of the windows.

"The fire is on the side of the house where the prisoner is!" cried Bert "It's in that secret corridor!"

"Maybe you'll have a chance to rescue him!" exclaimed the stenographer.

The fire had not gained much headway, and, under Bert's direction, a long ladder was procured, raised against the side of the house, and then, carrying the hose himself, the young chief ascended toward the blaze.

"Give me the stream!" called Bert to Cole, who was in charge of the engine.

From the nozzle came the white, frothy mixture. Bert directed it at the window through which the flames were coming.

"Don't you dare go in that hall!" shouted Muchmore, running from the side door of the house to the foot of the ladder. "The fire doesn't amount to much. You can put it out from where you are, young man. I never called your department out. The old woman got scared and sent in the alarm. It's only some rubbish burning."

"I'll do as I think best about putting the fire out," replied Bert.

"Don't you go in that corridor!" yelled Muchmore, who seemed frantic over something.

The chemical stream was already smothering the blaze, and Bert could go a little farther up the ladder. He continued on, coming right opposite the window. Then he knew it was the same casement from which the mysterious message had been thrown. He could look in now, and he saw that the fire came from a pile of rags and paper on the floor. He directed the chemical stream directly on them, and in a few seconds the last vestige of the blaze was out. But Bert did not descend.

He was peering into the dark corridor. Would he get a sight of the prisoner held there? He tried to pierce the darkness. Surely that was a movement, surely that was someone hurrying to the window.

Bert looked down. He caught one glimpse of Muchmore, in the light from a lantern Tom Donnell was carrying, rushing at the ladder, as if to upset it, and precipitate the boy on it to the ground, thirty feet below.

But in the same glance Bert saw his chums holding back the enraged man. There was another movement in the corridor. Then a gleam of light showed, and, to his surprise, Bert saw an old man, carrying a lamp, coming toward him. The man's hands were bleeding, his clothes were disheveled, and his hair and beard were matted, as if they had known neither comb nor brush for a long time.

"Save me! Save me!" cried the man. "Is the fire out? I started it to call help! I thought the firemen would come. Oh, save me!"

"You're all right," replied Bert. "There is no danger. The fire is all out."

"Yes, the fire is out. There is no danger from that. It is my rascally nephew whom I fear. Save me from him!"

"Your nephew? Who is he?" asked Bert, wondering what was about to happen.

"Alfred Muchmore. Have you seen him? Where is he? If he finds me talking to you, he'll lock me up again. He shoved me back in the room after I started the fire, but I broke through the door. See my hands! They are cut and bleeding!"

"Who are you?"

"Harris Stockton."

"What? The owner of this place?"

"Yes, my lad. The owner of the Stockton mansion, which my rascally nephew is trying to force me to convey to him, together with all my other property. He has compelled me to sign some deeds, but to-night I refused to give him any more of my property. He has kept me a prisoner here many months, for I am weak and sickly, and he is strong. That old woman helped him. Once before, there was a fire here, and I thought I might escape, but I could not. Then, last night, some people tried to break down the door, but he drove them away. To-night, when he left me for a while, I started this fire. I knew it could not do much damage, and I hoped it would bring me help. Thank God, it has! You will not let him shut me up again, will you?"

"Well, I guess not!" exclaimed Bert, as he climbed over the window sill, and entered the long hall that was part of the unfortunate man's prison. "He'll have to tackle the whole Lakeville fire department if he does. You're safe now, Mr. Stockton."

"Oh! I'm so glad! It seemed as if I never would be free again!"

"We'll soon have you in better quarters than this," went on Bert. He leaned out of the window and shouted:

"Hey, Mort! 'I've got him! I've got the mysterious prisoner. It's Mr. Stockton! Come on up, and bring some of the boys! Grab Muchmore, and hold him!"

Frank V. Webster

The rascally nephew heard the words which meant that his career was at an end. He had been struggling to break away from Tom Donnell and the stenographer, who were holding him, to prevent him from upsetting the ladder.

At Bert's words the enraged man, with a violent effort, managed to wrench himself loose. He fled, for he knew the game was up. But it may be added here that he was subsequently captured, and sent to prison for a long term.

Into the mysterious house rushed the young fire-fighters, with Mort at their head to show them the way. The partly shattered door leading into the corridor was quickly broken open, in spite of the protests of Mrs. Blarcum, who did not seem to understand that Muchmore had fled, and that the real owner of the mansion was again in possession. A little later the old woman disappeared and all trace of her was lost.

As for Mr. Stockton, he soon was in his own apartments, where he quickly removed the signs of his imprisonment. Then he told his story, briefly, to Bert and his chums.

Muchmore, it appeared, had always been a bad character, but he had told his uncle that he had reformed, and had begged his relative to give him a home. No sooner was he installed in the mansion than he began to scheme to get possession of it, and also what other property Mr. Stockton had. To this end he secretly administered to his aged relative a medicine which greatly weakened him. Then, when the old man was not capable of defending himself, Muchmore had shut him up in an unused part of the house. From then on the nephew's course became bolder.

He began his wild, gambling life, introducing some of his cronies into the mansion. He compelled Mrs. Blarcum to do as he wished by telling her Mr. Stockton was crazy, and had to be kept a prisoner. Muchmore's strange actions, when the young firemen were first at the house, was due to his fear lest they discover that Mr. Stockton was a prisoner in his own mansion.

Then Muchmore began to make out deeds and other papers, compelling his uncle, by threats of violence, to sign such as were necessary for his purpose. Mr. Stockton tried several times to escape, but the rascally nephew and housekeeper were too much for him. Once Mr. Stockton managed to get as far as the office where Mort Decker, under the direction of Muchmore, was in the habit of copying deeds. The stenographer was out at the time, and the office was deserted, and, as he could not find a pen, the old man used the typewriter to prepare the mysterious note Herbert found. He was disturbed before he could finish it, but he carried it away with him, and, at the first opportunity, threw it from the window.

But now he had no more to fear, thanks to the rescue by Herbert.

"I can't thank you enough," he said to the young chief. "But for you I might still be a prisoner."

"You helped yourself as much as we helped you," said Bert "It was a good idea, to think of starting that fire."

"Yes, it was the only thing I could think of. This place is so lonesome that persons seldom pass by, or I might have called to some of them, when I was well enough. Often I had to stay in bed for days at a time. I made the fire of some old papers and rags, and I had a pail of water ready to throw on it in case it got going too fiercely. Then Muchmore came and caught me, and locked me up. Oh, how I prayed that they might send in an alarm, and that the fire department would come, for I heard from the old housekeeper that a company had been started in addition to the old hand-engine corps."

"Yes, we think we have quite a fine department," said Herbert proudly.

"Well, you'll soon have a better one," said Mr. Stockton. "I want to show my appreciation in some way, and I'm going to buy a regular steam-engine for the town."

"But we'll need a water system for that," objected Bert.

"That will come. I am going to sell a lot of property I have, and put a water system in Lakeville. I've held on to my land too long. We'll develop this village, until the old inhabitants, like myself, won't know the place. And, when we have the new department, I want you boys to have a hand in running it."

Mr. Stockton was as good as his word. It took some time to make the improvements he suggested, but finally a fine water system was installed in the town, and the best steam fire-engine money could buy was presented to Lakeville, with the compliments of the aged millionaire. In this work he was aided by Mort Decker, whom Mr. Stockton appointed his secretary.

It needed horses to draw the steamer, and of course required men to operate it. But the boys were not forgotten. They still kept the chemical engines—and the smaller lads the hand-engines—and they were often called on to put out trifling blazes, and help at the larger ones.

Mr. Stockton did not forget what Bert had done for him. He owned a comfortable house with two acres of ground and a barn, on one of the side streets of the town, and one day he surprised the young fireman by handing him a legal-looking document.

"What is this?" asked the youth in surprise.

"A deed to a house on Cherry Street," answered the rich man. "The place is now yours, free and clear. You and your mother can move into it at any time."

"Why, I didn't expect this," stammered Bert.

"I know you didn't, my lad, but it is yours, nevertheless. I want to do something for you—and for that good mother of yours."

Of course, Bert and Mrs. Dare were very grateful. They moved into the house a month later, and found it a far more comfortable home than they had ever before enjoyed.

Lakeville is now quite a city. It has two steam fire-engines, instead of one, the taxpayers purchasing the second. And if you were to go there tomorrow, or any other day, for that matter, and ask for the chief of one of the finest small departments in the United States, you would be introduced to Herbert Dare. For, after he finished his schooling, he was unanimously selected to act in his former capacity. And here, wishing him all success in the field which he has chosen for himself, and hoping that he may help save many lives and much property, we will say good-bye to our young fireman and his loyal comrades.

Choose from Thousands of 1stWorldLibrary Classics By

A. M. Barnard
Ada Leverson
Adolphus William Ward
Aesop
Agatha Christie
Alexander Aaronsohn
Alexander Kielland
Alexandre Dumas
Alfred Gatty
Alfred Ollivant
Alice Duer Miller
Alice Turner Curtis
Alice Dunbar
Allen Chapman
Alleyne Ireland
Ambrose Bierce
Amelia E. Barr
Amory H. Bradford
Andrew Lang
Andrew McFarland Davis
Andy Adams
Angela Brazil
Anna Alice Chapin
Anna Sewell
Annie Besant
Annie Hamilton Donnell
Annie Payson Call
Annie Roe Carr
Annonaymous
Anton Chekhov
Archibald Lee Fletcher
Arnold Bennett
Arthur C. Benson
Arthur Conan Doyle
Arthur M. Winfield
Arthur Ransome
Arthur Schnitzler
Arthur Train
Atticus
B.H. Baden-Powell
B. M. Bower
B. C. Chatterjee
Baroness Emmuska Orczy
Baroness Orczy
Basil King
Bayard Taylor
Ben Macomber
Bertha Muzzy Bower
Bjornstjerne Bjornson

Booth Tarkington
Boyd Cable
Bram Stoker
C. Collodi
C. E. Orr
C. M. Ingleby
Carolyn Wells
Catherine Parr Traill
Charles A. Eastman
Charles Amory Beach
Charles Dickens
Charles Dudley Warner
Charles Farrar Browne
Charles Ives
Charles Kingsley
Charles Klein
Charles Hanson Towne
Charles Lathrop Pack
Charles Romyn Dake
Charles Whibley
Charles Willing Beale
Charlotte M. Braeme
Charlotte M. Yonge
Charlotte Perkins Stetson
Clair W. Hayes
Clarence Day Jr.
Clarence E. Mulford
Clemence Housman
Confucius
Coningsby Dawson
Cornelis DeWitt Wilcox
Cyril Burleigh
D. H. Lawrence
Daniel Defoe
David Garnett
Dinah Craik
Don Carlos Janes
Donald Keyhoe
Dorothy Kilner
Dougan Clark
Douglas Fairbanks
E. Nesbit
E. P. Roe
E. Phillips Oppenheim
E. S. Brooks
Earl Barnes
Edgar Rice Burroughs
Edith Van Dyne
Edith Wharton

Edward Everett Hale
Edward J. O'Biren
Edward S. Ellis
Edwin L. Arnold
Eleanor Atkins
Eleanor Hallowell Abbott
Eliot Gregory
Elizabeth Gaskell
Elizabeth McCracken
Elizabeth Von Arnim
Ellem Key
Emerson Hough
Emilie F. Carlen
Emily Bronte
Emily Dickinson
Enid Bagnold
Enilor Macartney Lane
Erasmus W. Jones
Ernie Howard Pie
Ethel May Dell
Ethel Turner
Ethel Watts Mumford
Eugene Sue
Eugenie Foa
Eugene Wood
Eustace Hale Ball
Evelyn Everett-green
Everard Cotes
F. H. Cheley
F. J. Cross
F. Marion Crawford
Fannie E. Newberry
Federick Austin Ogg
Ferdinand Ossendowski
Fergus Hume
Florence A. Kilpatrick
Fremont B. Deering
Francis Bacon
Francis Darwin
Frances Hodgson Burnett
Frances Parkinson Keyes
Frank Gee Patchin
Frank Harris
Frank Jewett Mather
Frank L. Packard
Frank V. Webster
Frederic Stewart Isham
Frederick Trevor Hill
Frederick Winslow Taylor

Friedrich Kerst
Friedrich Nietzsche
Fyodor Dostoyevsky
G.A. Henty
G.K. Chesterton
Gabrielle E. Jackson
Garrett P. Serviss
Gaston Leroux
George A. Warren
George Ade
Geroge Bernard Shaw
George Cary Eggleston
George Durston
George Ebers
George Eliot
George Gissing
George MacDonald
George Meredith
George Orwell
George Sylvester Viereck
George Tucker
George W. Cable
George Wharton James
Gertrude Atherton
Gordon Casserly
Grace E. King
Grace Gallatin
Grace Greenwood
Grant Allen
Guillermo A. Sherwell
Gulielma Zollinger
Gustav Flaubert
H. A. Cody
H. B. Irving
H.C. Bailey
H. G. Wells
H. H. Munro
H. Irving Hancock
H. R. Naylor
H. Rider Haggard
H. W. C. Davis
Haldeman Julius
Hall Caine
Hamilton Wright Mabie
Hans Christian Andersen
Harold Avery
Harold McGrath
Harriet Beecher Stowe
Harry Castlemon
Harry Coghill
Harry Houidini

Hayden Carruth
Helent Hunt Jackson
Helen Nicolay
Hendrik Conscience
Hendy David Thoreau
Henri Barbusse
Henrik Ibsen
Henry Adams
Henry Ford
Henry Frost
Henry James
Henry Jones Ford
Henry Seton Merriman
Henry W Longfellow
Herbert A. Giles
Herbert Carter
Herbert N. Casson
Herman Hesse
Hildegard G. Frey
Homer
Honore De Balzac
Horace B. Day
Horace Walpole
Horatio Alger Jr.
Howard Pyle
Howard R. Garis
Hugh Lofting
Hugh Walpole
Humphry Ward
Ian Maclaren
Inez Haynes Gillmore
Irving Bacheller
Isabel Cecilia Williams
Isabel Hornibrook
Israel Abrahams
Ivan Turgenev
J.G.Austin
J. Henri Fabre
J. M. Barrie
J. M. Walsh
J. Macdonald Oxley
J. R. Miller
J. S. Fletcher
J. S. Knowles
J. Storer Clouston
J. W. Duffield
Jack London
Jacob Abbott
James Allen
James Andrews
James Baldwin

James Branch Cabell
James DeMille
James Joyce
James Lane Allen
James Lane Allen
James Oliver Curwood
James Oppenheim
James Otis
James R. Driscoll
Jane Abbott
Jane Austen
Jane L. Stewart
Janet Aldridge
Jens Peter Jacobsen
Jerome K. Jerome
Jessie Graham Flower
John Buchan
John Burroughs
John Cournos
John F. Kennedy
John Gay
John Glasworthy
John Habberton
John Joy Bell
John Kendrick Bangs
John Milton
John Philip Sousa
John Taintor Foote
Jonas Lauritz Idemil Lie
Jonathan Swift
Joseph A. Altsheler
Joseph Carey
Joseph Conrad
Joseph E. Badger Jr
Joseph Hergesheimer
Joseph Jacobs
Jules Vernes
Julian Hawthrone
Julie A Lippmann
Justin Huntly McCarthy
Kakuzo Okakura
Karle Wilson Baker
Kate Chopin
Kenneth Grahame
Kenneth McGaffey
Kate Langley Bosher
Kate Langley Bosher
Katherine Cecil Thurston
Katherine Stokes
L. A. Abbot
L. T. Meade

L. Frank Baum
Latta Griswold
Laura Dent Crane
Laura Lee Hope
Laurence Housman
Lawrence Beasley
Leo Tolstoy
Leonid Andreyev
Lewis Carroll
Lewis Sperry Chafer
Lilian Bell
Lloyd Osbourne
Louis Hughes
Louis Joseph Vance
Louis Tracy
Louisa May Alcott
Lucy Fitch Perkins
Lucy Maud Montgomery
Luther Benson
Lydia Miller Middleton
Lyndon Orr
M. Corvus
M. H. Adams
Margaret E. Sangster
Margret Howth
Margaret Vandercook
Margaret W. Hungerford
Margret Penrose
Maria Edgeworth
Maria Thompson Daviess
Mariano Azuela
Marion Polk Angellotti
Mark Overton
Mark Twain
Mary Austin
Mary Catherine Crowley
Mary Cole
Mary Hastings Bradley
Mary Roberts Rinehart
Mary Rowlandson
M. Wollstonecraft Shelley
Maud Lindsay
Max Beerbohm
Myra Kelly
Nathaniel Hawthrone
Nicolo Machiavelli
O. F. Walton
Oscar Wilde

Owen Johnson
P.G. Wodehouse
Paul and Mabel Thorne
Paul G. Tomlinson
Paul Severing
Percy Brebner
Percy Keese Fitzhugh
Peter B. Kyne
Plato
Quincy Allen
R. Derby Holmes
R. L. Stevenson
R. S. Ball
Rabindranath Tagore
Rahul Alvares
Ralph Bonehill
Ralph Henry Barbour
Ralph Victor
Ralph Waldo Emmerson
Rene Descartes
Ray Cummings
Rex Beach
Rex E. Beach
Richard Harding Davis
Richard Jefferies
Richard Le Gallienne
Robert Barr
Robert Frost
Robert Gordon Anderson
Robert L. Drake
Robert Lansing
Robert Lynd
Robert Michael Ballantyne
Robert W. Chambers
Rosa Nouchette Carey
Rudyard Kipling
Saint Augustine
Samuel B. Allison
Samuel Hopkins Adams
Sarah Bernhardt
Sarah C. Hallowell
Selma Lagerlof
Sherwood Anderson
Sigmund Freud
Standish O'Grady
Stanley Weyman
Stella Benson
Stella M. Francis

Stephen Crane
Stewart Edward White
Stijn Streuvels
Swami Abhedananda
Swami Parmananda
T. S. Ackland
T. S. Arthur
The Princess Der Ling
Thomas A. Janvier
Thomas A Kempis
Thomas Anderton
Thomas Bailey Aldrich
Thomas Bulfinch
Thomas De Quincey
Thomas Dixon
Thomas H. Huxley
Thomas Hardy
Thomas More
Thornton W. Burgess
U. S. Grant
Upton Sinclair
Valentine Williams
Various Authors
Vaughan Kester
Victor Appleton
Victor G. Durham
Victoria Cross
Virginia Woolf
Wadsworth Camp
Walter Camp
Walter Scott
Washington Irving
Wilbur Lawton
Wilkie Collins
Willa Cather
Willard F. Baker
William Dean Howells
William le Queux
W. Makepeace Thackeray
William W. Walter
William Shakespeare
Winston Churchill
Yei Theodora Ozaki
Yogi Ramacharaka
Young E. Allison
Zane Grey